As a professional psychologist of more than twenty years, I have done everything from running my own practice to engaging some of the most brilliantly devious criminal minds while consulting for federal law enforcement. My career was about as adventurous as could be for somebody in my field. So naturally, in my later years, I did what every other tired professional does: I went into the cushy life of teaching at the university level. During this time, I took on a lofty role as the head of the Department of Abnormal Psychology at the University of Texas at Pemberton, where I enjoyed a tenured position and a more than generous research grant. Much of my research revolved around the human mind's ability to create complex delusions as a way of masking hard realities. In my studies, I have researched and spoken with abused children, victims of sex trafficking, people who had left cults, and survivors of what would have been very gruesome murders. But nothing I have seen has had as much of an impact on my own psyche or has been as much of a challenge as figuring out what happened to the Dunnhill's.

In order to help you, the reader, relive the ordeal of the Dunnhill family during what we refer to in the department as "The Long Night At 312 Derby Lane," I am forced to remove myself from its revelation to the public for a number of reasons, and place a surrogate in the role of the story teller. The Derby Lane case has been the most intimidating obstacle I have had to surmount in my years as a psychologist and a skeptic. Without definitive proof, eye witness accounts, police investigation, or media coverage, I originally found it more bogus than anything I have encountered, even in the realm of fiction, when conducting interviews in my research on post-traumatic stress involving supposed "supernatural" occurrences. My hypothesis was that the episodes experienced by my subjects were merely the mind's way of coping with extremely traumatic events. That the subjects had created a delusional fantasy in order to come to terms with something their fragile mental states could not handle.

A colleague of mine, who wishes to remain nameless to protect their reputation, was aware of my research and directed me to those involved with this particular case. I admit, there were not many. My initial thought was that what occurred could be explained in some rational way. Perhaps it was some cruel joke being played on the Dunnhill's, or a gas leak in the household bringing about hallucinations. However, after diving very deep into a private investigation (independent of my research) and traveling all over the world to connect broken pieces, I can no longer conclude that my original findings were accurate. To continue to be skeptical would place me in a position where I would become like my subjects, merely trying to reach beyond reality to convince myself that what I saw was not really what I saw. The reality of it is that what allegedly happened to the Dunnhill's did in fact happen, that the events of The Long Night are 100% true, and that the Dunnhill's story is not fiction. This reverse variable of my research has discredited me to the point where my study has been shut down, my funding has been pulled, and I am back to being merely another professor, my tenure having suddenly been yanked from me. I believe outside forces have made my downfall accelerate, and at this point I have nothing to lose anymore.

    And so, to honor the Dunnhill's, and to warn the public of the vile, horrific, and outright shockingly unbelievable things that are likely still occurring underneath our very noses, I believe it to be my moral obligation to continue to put everything I have worked so hard for my entire life on the line so that the truth of that night will finally be revealed. To weave such an outlandish tale in a manner that would do it justice would be beyond my capabilities. I decided the best way to convey what occurred at 312 Derby Lane was to create a sort of fictionalized narrative. While this may seem highly unorthodox (and counter-intuitive), I felt a boring case study would turn people away, and create more skepticism than belief. I also feel, due to those outside forces mentioned earlier, that it is more likely to be purchased (and not killed outright) if the consumer believes it is fiction. But make no mistake, ***this is not fiction***.

I now leave the telling of the Dunnhill's story in the capable hands of a good friend of mine, an aspiring writer named J Orion Liptak, whose oddball short stories I have thoroughly enjoyed during our time working together on this case. As my scribe for the last two years, Mr. Liptak was capable of conveying the terror and isolation felt by the Dunnhill's, and as such, much of this book will be directly based off of his own notes and writings into my research. I can only wish him the best of luck in this lofty endeavor. For the real reason I have decided to step away from this book truly comes to me as I finish writing this opening, and sift through the fragments of data that paint a truly horrific picture: That I am too afraid to tell the story myself, and I am so very tired of the nightmares.

Dr. Perry James Alton, Ph. D.

Professor of Abnormal Psychology, University of Texas at Pemberton

The Long Night At 312 Derby Lane

By J Orion Liptak

    As the sun rose above the rooftops of Derby Lane, Scott Dunnhill looked around and, as he did every Saturday morning, took stock of everything that most are too busy to appreciate or notice. He had promised himself, years ago, that he would do this every Saturday morning if he ever got his life in order. And he did. He strolled down the walkway to the road to grab the morning paper, and turned to look at his house. A stylish two story with dark red brick and gray-blue paneling, with new roof shingles and new electrical wiring. He had spent a whole week landscaping the front garden, and new bushes, roses, and various vines adorned the front porch, which stretched along almost the entire expanse of the front of the house. As Scott looked at the house that he and his family had worked so hard to make their home, he couldn't help but feel immense pride in himself. Dropping the paper on the front porch, he turned around again and continued his Saturday morning ritual of taking in the sights.

He looked down the street to the right, and then to the left. All of the houses on Derby Lane were nice two story houses, but each unique. Some had porches that hooked around the front and side of the house, some had screened in porches, and some merely had steps up to the door, with no porch at all. Scott liked porches. He insisted that he have some space to stretch out, and wouldn't buy a house without a comfortable porch. As he scanned the tree tops for squirrels and birds, memories of his days as a struggling artist flooded back into his mind. The tiny apartment, the canned meals, paper strewn across every inch of his floor, assaulted with designs, doodles, and incomprehensible scribbles that would make any passerby assume he was mad. No porch, no backyard. Just stuffed into a compartmentalized box in a city filled with people and devoid of humanity. The memory left his mind just as soon as it had entered. A hummingbird with beautiful blue, purple, and white plumage fluttered up to the porch of his home on the corner lot (colonial revival, the realtor called it), hovering next to the feeder and filling itself with sweet nectar. It was rather cool for a summer morning, and a thin layer of dew covered the lawn like an ethereal frost.

As Scott sipped his coffee, Mr. Harris, who lived in the corner lot across the street, came outside to get his morning paper. He waved to Scott, and

Scott smiled and waved back. A tall man with grayish hair, big glasses, and a large frame, Mr. Harris had lived in this neighborhood for many decades, and had seen many people come and go out of the corner house at 312 Derby Lane. A big smile spread across Mr. Harris' old face, and it seemed that he, like Scott, enjoyed his Saturday morning routine. He chuckled and turned to walk back inside his house, only turning once more to call his dog back in, who had just defecated on the curb. Scott turned his attention away from the unrefined brown turd that threatened to obstruct his peace and tranquility. Nothing would ruin this already perfect day. Across the street from Mr. Harris' house, diagonal from Scott's house on the corner lot, the large oak tree that sat in the front yard of the Monroe's house became an epic battle ground as two squirrels zigzagged up and down the tree, chittering and playing, possibly fighting over crumbs of food with the birds. Scott took a deep breath inward, and exhaled pure repose. From inside the house, he could smell the bacon sizzle on the stove, it's divine scent wafting out of the open windows. Before this, before the open blue sky, peaceful suburbia, large trees with emerald green leaves, and active nature, Scott lived in the city, crammed into a tiny efficiency apartment, smaller than his dorm room in college. No social life, no money, no happiness. There was something empty in young Scott, something that not even his art could fulfill. Unlike many artists, who manage to live the rest of their days hoping to God that something will land and stay in the big city as if it was their own personal Hell, Scott decided that he could be an artist anywhere, and moved to the smaller (but not too small) town of Fort Dalton, TX, started a family, then moved them to Pemberton where he took a job as a graphic designer for a mid level advertising firm, creating a tee shirt printing business on the side. Yes, Scott Dunnhill had sold out. And it was beautiful.

    The glass storm door opened, and Jason walked outside, still in his Batman pajamas. At ten years old, he was almost the full spitting image of Scott. Taller than most other kids, with brown medium length curly hair, and a little ball at the end of his nose. A small gap in his teeth would eventually close, Scott knew, but for now that meant Jason had a hard time whistling. It was amusing watching him try, of course, and Scott and Jason would often joke around about such things. Scott was very proud of Jason, and sometimes wondered how the Hell he lucked out so well. "Hey dad, mom says it's time for breakfast and that you need to get your buns in here before she gives all of our food to the homeless," said Jason. Jason took after his mother in other ways, particularly her snarky sense of humor.

"Your mother needs to chill." Scott elicited a laugh from Jason, and cracked a wry grin. Scott ruffled his son's hair and gestured for him to scoot inside. "Comb your hair before you sit down to eat, or your mother will think she's actually feeding the homeless." Scott marveled at this moment over his perfect life, and how happy everybody in the house was. It meant he was doing a good job.

"Fine," protested Jason, as he ran back into the house. Scott was about to follow suit when he heard somebody call to him. Scott was enjoying the Saturday morning routine so much, the sound almost scared him. Scott whipped around.

"He's getting pretty big!" shouted Mr. Harris from across the street. He had the biggest ear to ear grin you've ever seen, and his wrinkled eyes were almost slammed shut. His dog, already having ruined the equilibrium of the street, was struggling to race back into the house, fighting against the taut pull of the leash. An oblivious Mr. Harris didn't seem to notice though. He just stared straight forward, flashing that expensive dental work, his eyes squinting so tight, beaming with neighborly glee.

"Huh?" Scott was so immersed in his perfect little life, he had no idea what Mr. Harris was referencing.

"Your boy! Jason!" Mr. Harris shouted again. "He's getting very tall!"

Scott laughed. "Oh, yeah. Just turned ten. Give him another couple years, he'll be as tall as his old man."

Mr. Harris smile faded a little. "No. We wouldn't want that, now would we?" As if catching himself, Mr. Harris' toothy grin returned, his eyelids pushed against each other, and he chuckled and waved goodbye, then turned and walked inside.

Scott half smiled. It was a little strange to him how attentive his neighbors were towards Jason. Always wondering what he was doing when they came over, always asking how tall he was. *Were they obsessed with him*? He chuckled at the absurdity of the thought, then followed his son inside to eat breakfast.

The reality of the situation would prove to be too inconceivable for Scott Dunnhill to handle.

Andrea Dunhill didn't enjoy her Saturday's as much as her husband did.

This could possibly be because she was a stay at home mother. It could also be that she liked to spread her chores out over the week while Scott was at work, and had nothing to do on Saturday. Andrea liked to keep busy. And Saturday's at 312 Derby Lane were anything but busy. In fact, they were a day of social gathering, people coming and going, and a cause of much stress for Andrea, who could swear she now suffered from a crippling anxiety because of it. Of course, that could have a lot less to do with her mental or emotional state, and a lot more to do with the company that was kept.

Scott's friend's had wives, and their wives were Andrea's friends by default. They were catty at times, gossiped, and drank a little too much wine by the end of the afternoon. They all had a very light, almost aristocratic air to them that Andrea found to be annoyingly phony. She was always one of the boys growing up, and hardly had anything in common with these women. Andrea, like Scott, enjoyed her peace and quiet. Unlike Scott, she was not really a social butterfly. But she loved her husband, and wanted him to be happy. Besides, it was only one day out of the week. For three years. One day out of a week full of six other days with nothing but peace and quiet. Andrea thought to herself that this must be the suburban Hell that people talked about, and was hoping she wasn't just some upper middle class chick with first world problems.

That's not to say Andrea wasn't happy. In fact, she may have been happier than her husband, who regularly remarked how much better life has been for him since he retreated to a simpler life and met her. After all, she was a mother to an amazing boy who all of their friends doted on, and was married to an incredibly talented and attractive man who always provided for them. Andrea was content with things as they were, and remembered this as she sat there, sandwiched between a peculiar group of four women.

And there was certainly something so terribly artificial about these women. The way they laughed so hard at such little things, as if they were the funniest things in the world. Andrea would think to herself that nothing in the world was that funny. But she did try. Lord knows she put a big smile on her face, and pretended to laugh along. But as three years had passed, so too had her patience for this routine. As she suppressed the urge to pour some whiskey into her tea, Andrea sat on the sofa and listened to these women prattle on and on about God knows what. Music played in the background on a small Bluetooth speaker, and the men were outside on the back patio, drinking beer and giving Scott useless pointers on how to grill meat. Scott didn't need that, as he was a fantastic cook anyway, but maybe that's just what men do, thought Andrea. Drink beer and talk about their meat.

Jason played with the Maxwell's son, Chris, and the Branford's daughter, Jessica. The three have been practically inseparable for the last three years. They went to school together, built forts together, played in the woods together, and for the most part all were very normal, and fairly well behaved kids. The Maxwell's, Linda and Martin, were real estate agents who actually sold the Dunnhill's their peaceful little home on 312 Derby Lane for what can only be described as "highway robbery," as Scott would often joke. They were a younger couple, mid-thirties, much like Scott and Andrea, however their son Chris did not look anything like them, oddly enough. Jessica Branford, on the other hand, was adopted when she was just a baby, her parents having been struck by an 18 wheeler. Katie and Robert Branford were in their mid-fifties, and adopted Jessica because their own child had passed away years ago. They never seem to want to talk about it, and Andrea certainly had no itch to drudge up any painful memories. She was just happy that Jason was happy, and had well-adjusted friends. As different, in interests and activities, as these kids happened to be from Jason, they were nevertheless playing and studying together every single day.

"I said, Andrea, when are you going to get new curtains in here? These dark greys just don't let in a lot of light." Andrea snapped her attention away from her straying thoughts and back into the mindless conversation of her "friends." All of the women, from Katie Branford to Linda Martin in the easy chairs to Donna Harris and Bridgette Monroe on the sofa, were staring in anticipation at Andrea. She felt like she was on a slab having a live alien autopsy performed on her.

"Oh. Well, we wanted to go with a design that was cooling to the senses. We liked the grey tones because they invoke a quiet storm in the distance." Andrea kind of hated herself a little after saying that. Even though she was doing her best impression of a faux bourgeois suburban housewife, Andrea wanted nothing more than to smack the glass of wine out of Bridgette Monroe's hand. An aging trophy wife for her husband Wesley, a retired contractor, she had little white spots of what Scott would jokingly refer to as melanoma on her sun baked skin. You could tell that, at one point, she was quite beautiful, and the pictures in their house proved it. Most families would think it odd to have family photos in the hearth of their house featuring the lady of the house in a skimpy bikini, but then again, the mindset of a man who takes a wife so much younger than himself could be responsible for this. Wesley was certainly proud of Bridgette, as any accomplished person is of any trophy or reward they win in life. Unfortunately, the one thing Bridgette had going for her in life was slowly fading away.

Bridgette waved her hand in dismissal at Andrea. "Nonsense, for as often as you have us over, some color will brighten the mood in this place. Let me call my interior decorator, Jonah. He can come out tomorrow at the earliest to at least give you an estimate." Bridgette pulled out her cell phone, and her long, fake fingernails struggled to swipe the screen. She looked like a fingerless monkey trying to use chopsticks.

Andrea hated it when the other wives, particularly Bridgette, "insisted" on pressuring her to do something she had no desire to do. Andrea wasn't very good at saying no. Perhaps it was something in her upbringing. Perhaps there was something that happened in her past that could have caused a negative association with the word. In the three years that the Dunhill's had inhabited 312 Derby Lane, the walls had been painted, the furniture rearranged, the décor restructured, even the floors were a solid hardwood (Mrs. Harris insisted they were easier to clean stains off of). And after three years of caving and not allowing herself a little bit of control over her own home, Andrea was finally going to insist on keeping things the way she wanted them.

As the other women chatted gleefully about colors, hanging lights, pull ropes, and other such boring subjects, Andrea attempted to rise over the chorus and proclaim her lack of intent to change. "It's really not necessary, I like our current-" But it was too late. That fingerless monkey called Bridgette found the means to tap and was already calling the interior designer. Just about every Saturday, for almost three years, Andrea had put up with a lot. Her peaceful week, habitually thrown into a hole to appease her husband and son. Friends by default one day a week with the Stepford Wives. Andrea always feared she would become one. The passive aggressiveness. The blathering gossip. The inane chatter about drapes, and dresses, and doilies. Andrea had no idea specifically what could have prompted her to lose her cool at this very instant, but it all happened just the same. "Bridgette, put your phone away, I don't want to see your stupid interior whatever, I like my house the way it is and you should too!" Andrea was speaking loudly through her teeth, body clenched in frustration. If you stuck a pin in her arm, she would pop.

The area around the couch in the living room went into a vacuum where sound and movement did not exist. The children, distracted with their play, stopped running around and stared, mouths gaped open, at Andrea. This was uncharacteristic. And uncharacteristic was not something that happened at 312 Derby Lane. Bridgette looked taken aback. Her eyes blinked, then went wide open, and the right side of her mouth contorted downwards as her head followed, as if a giant fish hook was pulling her lips to her shoulder, which managed to cringe upwards. She placed her phone down on the end table next to her, and, perhaps instinctively, slowly reached for a butter knife that happened to be within arms reach. She grasped the knife in her hand and was about to slide it off the table into the air had it not been for Donna Harris placing her hand over Bridgette's. "Now dear," said Mrs. Harris, "this is not the time to do anything out of turn."

  Andrea couldn't believe what she had just seen. Was Bridgette Monroe actually going to pick up a butter knife and try to stab or cut her? Andrea didn't look like much at 5'3", but as stated, she was a tomboy growing up, and could handle herself very well. Bridgette never took her eyes off of Andrea. She slowly released her grip from the knife, which touched down softly on the table. Her head still tilted backwards, her eyes still wide as dinner plates and fixated on Andrea, Bridgette breathed in quick, quiet, successive bursts. The social backhand she was just dealt appeared to put her into a state of momentary paralysis, and suddenly it was as if a survival instinct kicked in where the only thing she knew to do was play the victim and become defensive. She put her hands up, palms outward as if to guard herself from whatever may come next. She blinked several times as if she had just been slapped in the face and was seeing stars. "Well... Andrea, you don't have to be rude about it."

Andrea couldn't quite believe it either. Normally she was very supportive of her boys' social lives, even if it caused her to hate that one day out of her week, and would never do anything to ruin her relationship with the neighbors. After all, while they were regularly odd in the way they said and did things, almost like adults in training, they had always been very good to the Dunnhill's. Andrea immediately apologized, although after the knife incident, she really didn't know why. "I'm... I'm sorry, Bridgette. I don't know what came over me." She felt like she was falling at that moment. Like an anvil had been chained to her ankle and she was just dropping at top speed into a bottomless pit.

Bridgette stood up and grabbed her clutch, looking too angry to burst into tears. "I'm leaving."

She said, matter of factly. She walked over to the back patio door, and did what Andrea dreaded she would do: She went to her husband and made a scene. The other women were meekly quiet as Bridgette, tears streaming down her face, poured her emotions out to her husband, tattling like a school child. The men outside all looked into the house to assess the situation, and Scott did not look too pleased. Wesley, trying to remain polite, consoled his wife, and then just to add to the ever so awkward situation, all of the men came inside to see what the commotion was about. After all, Andrea knew, men liked to solve problems.

"Is everything okay?" Scott walked in first, playing up the role of the calm head of the household, likely to defuse the situation before it went horribly wrong. His brow was terse, and Andrea seemed to get the feeling that he might not have her back.

"It's... It's nothing, sweetie. I just lost my cool is all. I didn't even mean to." Andrea wasn't paying enough attention, but the other women were all sipping their drinks, exchanging glances, and almost telepathically condemning Andrea. The bitter looks on their faces did not go unnoticed by Scott, whose brow furrowed even further at his wife.

Wesley was being a sport about it, for the most part. "Look, I'm going to take her home," he said. He put his arm around his wife, who glared at Andrea with such scorn, her eyes almost set the house aflame. Bridgette shook as if the house was twenty degrees. Andrea understood why Bridgette would be a bit upset, after all how could she have known Andrea was so upset about something like home décor, but was she so emotionally unbalanced that she could lose herself in this manner? Or was she drunk? Andrea became aware of the other women looking at her, glancing amongst themselves. This must have been how Julius Caesar felt the moment before his life ended. Before his trusted friends turned on him, each waiting to take a stab. Their eyes burned into her skull, lips pursed tightly together so not a drop of emotion could seep out. Did none of them notice the knife?

Sensing the awkwardness and hoping to cauterize the social wound before it bled out all over the living room, Scott decided they all had enough excitement for one day. "Actually, I think it's a good idea for us to end the day here." He shot a disappointed look towards Andrea again, who felt ashamed of herself. But why? For asserting control over her own house? "I think it just got a little crazy in here." Probably not the best way to put it, but then again, Scott wasn't exactly a statesman. What he probably would have said, had he the wherewithal, was "Folks, I think emotions are running a bit high right now, so why don't we take this opportunity to gather ourselves and reconvene at a later date." Something that diplomatic would certainly have saved the moment. Looking back on it, one must wonder if the events that transpired later that night were spurred on by this very moment, or if it was all inevitable, and Andrea's outburst and Scott's dismissal just moved up the timetable.

"Crazy? Crazy?! Are you calling me crazy?!" Bridgette broke away from Wesley's embrace and confronted Scott.

"No, Bridgette, not at all, I was just saying…" But Scott couldn't finish.

"You want to see crazy?!" Bridgette pointed to Andrea. "Who gets upset over curtains! Huh?! Curtains!" Wesley tried to console his wife, but she wasn't having any of it. "No! No! They're just curtains! And you had the audacity to scream and yell at me over curtains!"

"Bridgette, I didn't scream and yell at you…" Andrea also couldn't finish her sentence.

"Oh, so what, now I'm a liar too?! Liar and crazy?! How dare you! You owe me an apology! Right now!"

"I did apologize…" It was no use.

"You need to calm down, Andrea! Okay?! You need to calm down! You need to put your fists down, for your son! Your son is watching you, and he's learning bad habits from you, and he's not going to be ready! Do you hear me?! He won't be ready, and it'll be your fault! You better not ruin your son, Andrea!" Spit was flying out of Bridgette's lips as she screamed and ranted. "Jason means a lot to us, and I won't let you fuck anything up!" Andrea was speechless. Wesley just stood there, hanging his head and letting her get it out of her system. Scott, in a state of shock, could only stand between Bridgette and Andrea to avoid a fist fight starting in his living room. "I love Jason! Do you hear me? We all *love* Jason! And you aren't doing him any good! He needs more time!" Tears poured down her face, and her smeared makeup made her look like an aging, psychotic clown.

Wesley suddenly tried to shush Bridgette and grabbed hold of her, trying to usher her out the door. "And you'd better change those curtains! Do you hear me?! You'd better change those curtains!"

Wesley successfully ushered Bridgette out the door, and suddenly, it was very quiet.

"Yeah, I need everybody to leave." Scott had no idea what else to say.

"You mean, all of us?" Martin sounded torn apart.

"Yeah, I'm thinking everybody should just go on home, and maybe we can pick this all back up next week when everybody has had time to collect themselves." Scott didn't want to alienate his neighbors, but he knew the right thing to do would be to stand firm with his wife, especially after what he just saw. The energy in the room changed, and Scott got the feeling his neighbors were not happy with being so abruptly kicked out. As awkward as the situation that Andrea made was, Scott knew at that moment that he hadn't made it any better. As a matter of fact, as he looked around and saw the ashamed, scornful looks on everybody's faces, Scott knew he would likely have to make new friends. Why wasn't anybody condemning Bridgette for that? These people were weird.

"Chris wanted Jason to come stay the night at our house tonight!" Linda almost blurted the words out, with an odd sense of what Scott would later realize was desperation. As poorly timed as it was, it was even more suspicious the way her eyes darted around to find Martin, who was standing right next to her. Chris seemed confused at first. Linda gave her son an almost panicked, wide eyed glance. He looked to his mother, then back at Scott.

"Yeah. Can he? Please?" Chris pleaded innocently. Scott and Andrea didn't want to be those parents whose kids can't hang out with their friends because the parents don't get along. But in light of what just happened, Scott didn't think it would be a good idea for Jason to be over.

"Maybe tomorrow night, Chris. Tonight I think we're going to stay in." Scott lied. He lied right to a child's face. He had no idea if he was ever going to speak with these people again. Why hadn't any of them said something? Anything? For that matter, why hadn't he?

Chris looked at his parents, who shot him a glare normally reserved for a wicked child. Andrea wondered just what the Hell was going on. "But tomorrow is a school night." Chris looked from his parents back at Scott, his eyes almost filling up with tears, and seemed adamant that Jason stay the night. If Scott had given him three more seconds, Chris looked like he would have begged on his knees.

"Maybe next week, Chris. I'm sorry. I really am. We're gonna clean up and... Unrile ourselves." He looked at Andrea as he said this, slightly tense.

"You guys have a good evening though. And once again, I'm really sorry about this." Scott ushered their guests out the door. As unsettling as the stiff silence that weighed down the room was, nothing was more disconcerting than Linda Maxwell staring at Jason like a piece of meat as she walked out the door, tightly gripping her son's hand as it turned dark purple.

As Scott closed the door behind the Dunnhill's guests, Andrea squirmed uncomfortably, rubbing her upper arms as if she was cold. She knew this was not going to be a peaceful evening. The combination of the meltdown they just witnessed and the oddball reactions of their guests made her so uneasy she could hardly think. Scott, it seemed, was in the exact same mindset, albeit still angry with his wife. He walked back into the room, looked at his wife, and, in an accusatory manner, said "Well, that was weird."

Unbeknownst to them, it was the understatement of a lifetime.

They fought that evening.

They fought about the neighbors. They fought about miscommunication. They fought about alone time, and the meaning of happiness. They even fought about barbecue.

They fought about everything, it seemed.

Jason listened as his parents fought, forehead leaned against the staircase about halfway between the first and second floor. His legs were tucked under him, and his hands gripped the railing tightly, making him look like a little convict. They didn't even seem to notice him, or if they did, they didn't seem to care that he was there. He wasn't used to seeing his parents fight. They bickered, sure, but it was always very playful. This time, they were shouting, pointing, his dad even kicked a lamp over. Jason didn't even know that his mother was unhappy, and was alarmed as she tearfully poured her heart out to his father, who calmed down somewhat, taking on a more somber demeanor. Jason wanted to run to his mother and hug her, but something kept him from moving. Like maybe it would make the situation more awkward. Jason watched plenty of television and knew that, sometimes, you have to let people vent. He kept telling himself that this is what his parents were doing: Venting.

Jason wished he was at his friend's house right now, playing video games, laughing about things that would get him grounded if his parent's overheard. He didn't even mind answering Chris' weird questions. "Do you know what your blood type is? Mine is A." The weirdest ones began with "Would you..." and was usually filled with some very strange, somewhat disturbing act, often sexual in nature, followed by "...for a million dollars?" Jason would usually answer these with little to no honesty as a joke, yet Chris always seemed very intrigued at the answers, and would want to explore them even further.

Jason remembered this as his parent's fight calmed down over their agreement that their neighbors were, in fact, quite strange. Even at ten years old, Jason could tell that the fight centered around the neighbors, possibly before his parents even figured it out. And Jason agreed. While he had known his friends for three years (a near eternity for a child), he always felt a little uneasy around them. There was something about Chris and Jessica that Jason didn't like. It seemed, much like his mother, he was keen to play nice to appease his father, who was getting along very well with everybody else. But Jason's friends had a way of pushing him to do things he didn't want to do, manipulating him and, Jason suspected, even changing the way he thinks and feels about things. It was unnerving, and apparently his mother felt the same way.

Jason recalled a time he and his friends went into the woods. Their neighborhood was interwoven in a large park system, and wooded areas were very easy to come by. It was a very quick 5 minute walk to get to the nearest wooded area, with paths carved by Chris and Jessica when they were much younger. On this particular day, they were doing their usual walk and pretending they were on an alien world inhabited by giants, and the woods were the only safe place for them to hide. Jessica broke the dynamic of the fantasy world by pointing out a squirrel sitting on a tree branch, and coaxed Chris to throw a rock at it. Ever the hesitant one, Chris declined repeatedly, even with Jessica trying to sweet talk him into doing so. Jessica had a kind of power over the boys, as girls sometimes do. Each one wanted to gain her favor and impress her with various deeds. Without even thinking about it, Jason's instinct to outdo Chris and make Jessica happy kicked in and he picked up a large grey rock. It was an almost out of body experience, as if his soul wasn't attached to him, when he hurled the rock through the air, instantly knocking the squirrel to the ground below. Chris was startled, and immediately Jason felt a deep regret and dread for what he had done. Jessica remained calm, assuring them that everything was okay, and that they couldn't let the squirrel die for no reason.

They surrounded the squirrel, and Jessica knelt down in front of it. Chris and Jason followed suit, and the three of them formed a circle around the dead animal, laying in the pile of leaves. "We need to eat it's flesh." The words that came out of Jessica's mouth were more surreal to Jason than his first time killing another living thing. The look he gave her wasn't enough to break her, however. Jason was hoping there was a cruel joke in this, but she did not waver. Jason looked at Chris, who sat there on his knees, staring down at the squirrel in a trance. Jason knew he would get no backup from Chris, and looked back at Jessica in desperation.

"We can't do that, Jessica. It's insane. Isn't it?" Reasoning with her didn't seem to help his situation much. He looked back at Chris, but nothing had changed. Jason was doing everything he could to refrain from crying. Even after it all, he still didn't want Jessica to see him cry.

"Well, you killed it." Jessica said accusingly. "You can't let it go to waste. It's going to decompose, and rot. We have to eat it." Jessica looked him in the eyes, and he became lost inside of her gaze, cruel and caring at the same time. There is a psychological term for this known as conditioning. It is when one subject puts another subject through traumatic events, then coaxes them into a safe mentality. This ultimately builds a hierarchy of trust between the subjects, with one subject being dominant over the other. As the second subject's will breaks, they become easily suggestible. But Jason didn't know this. How could he? He was just a child. "Eat it." Jessica softly chanted. "Eat it." She picked up the dead squirrel and put it in Jason's hand. It was cold and hard, not fluffy and soft and warm as you would expect. Jessica closed his fingers over the squirrel's body, and was about to force his hand to snap the neck and rip open the carcass when Chris swatted at a fly and Jason, frightened, pulled away from Jessica and ran off through the forest.

She had implored him later, as she always had, to keep it a secret. And, as always, he did.

Jason knew it would be difficult to sleep tonight what with his parents at odds, and the memories of the woods that day, and a flood of other memories of similar strange and disturbing moments. Jason watched plenty of TV and wondered if Jessica may be a serial killer. It was the first time, oddly enough, that this thought had crossed his mind. He attempted to erase those images from his mind, as he so often did, while brushing his teeth and preparing for bed. Things had finally calmed down, and maybe it wouldn't be so bad after all. Maybe now that his mother had yelled at Mrs. Monroe, he wouldn't have to be friends with Jessica anymore.

Both of his parents came to tuck him in to start that long night at 312 Derby Lane. A showing of solidarity, perhaps. But all the same, it was welcome. The lights went out, and Jason drifted off into sleep. Not a deep sleep, it would seem. But a light sleep, the kind that leads into dreams and nightmares. A light sleep abruptly interrupted by the crackling and beeping of a 2 way radio on Jason's desk, shared with Chris at his insistence and always on when they weren't together.

"Jason. Jason! Come in. Please." Chris' whispered voice jolted Jason out of his light sleep. Jason looked at the alarm clock as he shuffled his way to the desk against the opposing wall. It was only 10:30. Half an hour of sleep that felt like at least a few, and Jason's eyes were heavy. He wanted to sink back into bed and ignore Chris, as it was likely just an invite to sneak out and pal around the street for a bit. "Jason, it's urgent. I don't have a lot of time. Please."

Jason grabbed the mic. "Dude, I just went to sleep. What is it?"

"You have to get out of there, Jason. Please. I'm sorry for everything, I really am. I had no choice." Chris's voice was beginning to shake as he spoke in harsh whispers.

"What are you talking about? What's happening?" Jason's confusion was fighting with his weariness.

"They're coming for you. Oh geez, I hope they aren't there yet. You should still have some time if you just go now." Chris wasn't making any sense.

"Go? Go where?" Chris was playing a joke on him, he must have been.

"I don't know. I'm sorry Jason, I really... I don't know, but you just have to go. Nowhere is safe, but you have to believe me, please." Chris' voice had even more desperation in it, if that was possible. It sounded like he was crying.

"Chris, is everything okay?" Jason was starting to worry.

"It's too late for me. But I couldn't just..." Chris was cut off by a loud sound, as if a door had just opened and banged loudly against the wall. The sound was so loud and sharp, Jason jumped and dropped the mic on the floor. A screeching roar emanated from the speaker, followed by the quick scream of a child, then static filled the air, cutting through what was supposed to be a very quiet, peaceful night.

    Jason panicked, and didn't even grab anything he might find useful. Didn't even think to go wake his parents. He just didn't think. He opened the window, and the surprisingly cool summer air flooded into the otherwise warm second floor room. He was in such a hurry, he didn't even catch a glimpse of it. Not until he stepped out of the window and brushed it with his foot.

The little anthropomorphic bear cubs were just let out of the little jail where they had been kept for some undisclosed time for some undisclosed reason. It didn't really matter. Jovial and eager to return home, they climbed on their bikes and rode down the street, to the poor part of town, to the tiny wooden house with the little dirt driveway. Momma and Pop bear awaited their return with smiles and hugs. They ran inside the house, excitedly entering the threshold. Wait, why were these sweet little anthropomorphic bear cubs in jail? Like I said, it didn't matter. None of this did, for the most part.

The inside of the house was much larger than it seemed on the outside, and resembled an old abandoned slaughterhouse, made up to look like a colonial cabin. To the left, a long and wide section with straw on the hard floor, and a massive barn style door on the far end. Along the wall, several cubbies were carved into the wall, which the cubs ran to and grabbed snacks from. They ran to the right and climbed a small set of wooden stairs to another section of the slaughterhouse, with rows of old rocking crib beds like you used to see in the old cartoons. A railing separated the upper section from the larger lower section.

The cubs circled their Gramma bear. Her grainy, deeper, yet sweet voice humored the cubs when they offered her their sweets, and she chuckled and made slow attempts at getting the cubs into bed, as if cherishing the moment she was having with them. The cubs climbed on her and begged her to take some of their crackers, or cookies, but she just assured them that it was time to go to bed. Without warning, she suddenly snapped her attention to an unseen entity in the slaughterhouse. If it had been you, or me, she would be looking us directly in the eyes, not a foot from our faces. Her voice, once matronly, was now vicious, a loud hiss, yet booming with southern bravado. "Fool! You've let evil into your home! It's too late for you, but you can still save the boy!" As she said this, fully grown anthropomorphic bears rose out of the rocking cribs, slowly, with menacing faces, directing their attention towards the eyes of this unseen entity, which, as I said, could very well be you or me. The bears were all chanting, a haunting, taunting chant: "Ha ha ha ha. Ha ha ha ha."

Repeatedly, droning, over and over, louder and louder. Their eyebrows furrowed, the whites of their eyes visible from the other side of the slaughterhouse. The bears walked slowly, slightly hunched, toward the entity, advancing behind Gramma bear, who continued her hasty warning. "Such little time you have left now, don't let it go to waste!" As the taunting chant grew louder and louder, Gramma bear raised her voice to a yell, loud enough to barely be heard over the noise. "There's a monster outside your window!"

Shaking.

"There's a monster outside your window!" The screech of what sounded like a violin cut through the air.

"Ha ha ha ha. Ha ha ha ha."

Pulling.

"There's a monster outside your window!" Her voice started taunting now.

The whole place moved violently back and forth.

"Ha ha ha ha."

"There's a monster outside your window!"

"Ha ha ha ha." Their broad shoulders shook as they laughed in their pulsating cadence. Closer and closer they moved.

The rooftop crumbled, and light came pouring in like fire.

"There's a monster outside your window!"

"Wake up."

"Huh? Wha?"

"Dad, wake up." Jason whispered in the night. A little flash light from a toy spy kit was shining in Scott's face, and Jason was shaking his father awake.

"What is it, son?" Scott's eyes were pressed shut with sleep. He couldn't see the boys lip quiver erratically, couldn't see the tears welling up in his eyes, but he could sense the fear and desperation in his son's voice.

"There's a monster outside my window."

Scott had been a father for ten years now. There were a number of times that he had to look for monsters under the bed, in the closet, and yes, even outside of the window. Every time, the same thing: A shoe, a jacket, a squirrel. He couldn't even remember the last time he had to do "the monster check." So to say that he was embarrassed that his ten year old son was clutching his arm in fear at this very moment was a given. Making his way down the hall, he tried to come up with a way to comfort his son while still remaining firm. He didn't want Jason to grow up soft, after all, and ten years old was too old to believe in monsters.

Ten years of parenting culminated in this very crucial moment.

Scott thought of the dream he just had as Jason cowered behind him. Why bears? Did he see a movie with bears? Did he see a Berenstain Bears book somewhere? Is there some deeper psychological reason for bears being present in the dream? And why were they anthropomorphic? In psychology, bears in your dreams tend to represent many things, namely the cycle of life and death, as well as a tendency towards habit. They can also signify close family bonds, in particular ones of a protective nature. Perhaps Scott's subconscious was warning him about something life threatening. Perhaps the breaking of his peaceful Saturday routines was lingering in his mind, driving him mad in his sleep. Perhaps, most likely, something was going to happen, and he needed to take action to protect his loved ones. Those familiar with "the long night" like to think, given the complex nature of the dream, that it was all three. That something about the awkward debacle from earlier set a warning sign off in his head. Of course, Scott would not know any of this. How could he? He was just a graphic designer. He was so tired he forgot the questions the moment he asked them. He was even so worn out he almost forgot to open the door to Jason's room, coming inches from bumping into it. He fumbled in the dark for the door knob, finally grasping it in his tired hand. Why did Jason shut the door?

Oh, right. Monster.

The door creaked open and Scott entered first, with Jason following closely behind, shining his little toy flashlight all over the room, filling the corners with pathetic amounts of light. Scott went to the desk to turn on the lamp, and tripped on the microphone that Jason had only a minute ago dropped on the ground. "Jesus, son, I told you to clear your floor!" Scott reached the desk and clicked on the little desk lamp, allowing just enough light in to have a good look around.

Jason whipped his head quickly around the room. "I'm sorry dad, but I was sleeping and I got a call from Chris and he said I was in danger and had to leave fast and then there was this noise and he disappeared so I went out the window and that's where the monster was." Jason, as most children have a tendency to do when excited, was talking so fast he wasn't even breathing. Scott recalled a time when he was a teenager living in Fort Dalton with his parents, and his friend called him in the middle of the night to tell him he had seen a UFO. Scott, like most people whose friend tells them they saw a UFO, was completely dismissive. It turned out, many people in their group of friends and family saw the phenomenon in the sky that night, and it was certainly unexplainable. Bright lights sashaying through the dark sky, like multicolored fireballs, spinning around each other in intricate patterns like two figure skaters who could never touch, but desperately wanted to. Fort Dalton has many odd stories like this, and Scott kicked himself for years after at the thought of missing such a life changing moment because of his closed mindedness. Looking back, perhaps that is why he chose to investigate the matter, and humor his son. Or perhaps it was the bear dream.

The thought left Scott's mind quickly as he realized what Jason had just said. "You tried to go out the window? Son, you could have fallen and died! You could have broken something!" Scott was more worried than he was angry, but it's often difficult to show that when you're a dad. Why was he trying to sneak outside? Jason would never do that. Would he?

"I'm sorry, dad. But I had to make sure Chris was okay." Jason looked like he was going to cry. Scott felt for him, he really did. He found his patience again, realizing that, as a father, it was his job to guide his son in the right direction, and not admonish him for his errors.

"He was probably playing a joke on you, son." Scott looked from Jason to the window, exhaling in both frustration and relief that his son was not hurt. The faint outline of a tree swayed to and fro outside of it, with just enough glare from the desk lamp to make it slightly difficult to see outside. Of course Jason was scared, thought Scott. He was a little freaked out by it himself. "See? It's a tree, son. You brushed up against a tree. Now let's get you some water and back into bed, kid." Scott ushered Jason softly by the shoulder towards the bedroom door.

"But dad, there isn't a tree outside my bedroom window," said Jason.

The realization hit Scott hard, and he turned his head back around just in time to see the thing outside the window slowly rake it's long, spindly, branch like fingers across the glass and walk out of view.

"What the...?" Scott ran to the window to see what just walked past, but by the time he could press his face against the left side of the panel and crane his eyeballs towards the right side, it was gone. His breath fogged the window in front of his face, and he quickly wiped it away.

"Dad? What was it?" Jason did not see it walk away, but could see that it was gone, and knew, by his father's fear, that something was definitely wrong.

Scott just stared out the window for a moment, hoping it would walk back into view. *My God, it was huge*, he thought. "I don't know, son."

Jason trembled. "What's going on?"

Scott shushed Jason but didn't divert his attention away from the window. He was hoping he could hear something, or get some sign of life. He found himself whispering. "Jason, turn off the desk lamp." Jason hesitated, but then edged towards the lamp, shaking with fear. The desk lamp clicked, and Scott was able to see through the window more clearly. He couldn't quite make it out, but there was something off at the edge of the house, along the fence line. Something unfamiliar.

"Scott?" Scott almost jumped when Andrea burst into the room, in just her bathrobe and night gown. He and Jason both shushed her. "What are you doing?" she asked, only to be shushed again. She turned to Jason. "Why are you up so late?" This time she whispered, so as not to be silenced for a third time.

Jason didn't move, but whispered "There's something outside." Andrea's head turned from Jason to Scott at the window. She slowly approached Scott, who did not turn away from the window.

"Scott?" she whispered. "Honey? What are you looking at?" Without warning, Scott turned and hurried out of the room, almost knocking her over. She quickly followed him, completely forgetting her son, who followed both of them for fear of being left alone in the pitch black dark.

Scott ran downstairs as fast as he could, his footsteps pounding across the house. He leapt past the last three steps and almost tripped, only barely catching himself along the wall. He used the momentum of catching himself to continue moving along the wall, finally maintaining his balance on the way to the back door. Andrea came down the stairs, quickly yet lightly, and Jason followed closely behind, carefully treading the steps so as not to fall and crash into his mother.

Scott made it to the back door and flipped the light switch that turned on the back patio light. The light was not the brightest, and if Scott could believe what he was seeing, he wasn't seeing much of it. They were crawling over the back fence, slowly. Creeping over, careful not to disrupt a single splinter of wood or blade of grass. Long, spindly arms attached to sharp, tendril like fingers and no legs, barely caressing the ground as the monster attached to it slithered over the panel, a long, skeletal tail protruding from the back, accented with a large, blade-like talon. To the left, what looked like a six armed, white skinned man in a suit skittered over the top of the fence, his entire face covered with 6 massive, human like eyeballs and gnashing pincers, slobbered with drool, where his mouth should have been. His fingers, about a foot long each, moved independent of his hands, as if snake-like, and as all of his 6 foot long legs touched the ground, knees bent upwards like a spider, his fingers rapidly moved his whole body behind the tree in the back. Fingers that looked like hairy spider's legs. A hulking monster made entirely of mud poured itself upwards out of the ground, forming some kind of golem like figure, roughly 8 feet tall. It's slanted red eyes stuck out from the oozing black and brown muck, and a gap opened up in the middle where wide, flat teeth were illuminated by a glowing orange presence inside of it's mouth.

Further to the right, more monsters poured over the fence, slowly, menacingly. Some with scales, some with leathery skin, and some seemingly turned inside out, their flesh exposed to the air. Their appendages were not to proportion, and one in particular had a long neck, bulbous head, and round glowing yellow eyes. As a matter of fact, many of them did, however they seemed to be covered in shadow. They could have been mistaken for humans at a distance, except the way they moved was a revolving set of slow and fast movements, like they were being sped up at random intervals. There must have been dozens of shadow people, all with long, outstretched arms, necks, and torsos, slowly moving towards the back door, their incandescent, creepy eyes all fixated on Scott.

Scott thought of the dream. *Ha ha ha ha.*

Scott was too horrified to close the door. If he had his wits about him, he would have closed the door and spared his family this traumatic sight. He would have shielded his son from seeing these creatures, and spared him the sense of impending doom that fell over the house. But in truth, Scott was too afraid. Too mesmerized by the scene unfolding in front of him. And so, he stood there in the door frame, mouth agape, as monsters came pouring slowly over the back fence like an overflowing sink, his wife and son watching over his shoulder. Scott only came to his senses when he saw the monster outside of Jason's window round the corner of the house, roughly twenty feet tall with a bark-like exoskeleton, large sinister glowing eyes, and a giant mouth carved deep into it's body with razor sharp teeth brandished into a twisted smile. It bounded towards Scott, it's gigantic, desk sized hand reaching out to grab him. Scott panicked and slammed the door shut, locking both locks in the process. He pressed his body against the door, and pointed to the couch. "Slide the couch over here! Now!" Andrea and Jason struggled to push the couch to the back door as the behemoth pounded on the back door, demanding they come out, it's angry voice booming against the silence of the night. They barricaded the door shut, unaware of the futility of their actions.

"What's happening, Scott?!" Andrea was about one step away from a nervous breakdown. Eventually, it was concluded that she did not have the time to process the situation as Scott and Jason had, given that she walked into the situation late.

"We have to get out of here!" Scott rushed everybody to the front door, hoping they could make a beeline to the car and escape. Scott grabbed the keys off the key ring next to the front door, almost ripping the holder out of the wall, and threw the door open.

This, too, would prove futile.

To the Dunnhill's horror, the street was filled with a line of grotesque, deformed, distorted, and deranged beasts. Hulking, intimidating, but not moving forward, they formed a blockade of fear, dashing all hopes of a swift escape. The street light showed what little could be seen. A tall, thin man with brittle strands of hair wearing an open trench coat, green, putrid gas pouring out of his open chest, and large spiders crawling all over his body stood in front of the others. His stomach stood out from the rest of his body, a round belly bigger than two basketballs, and Scott couldn't help but notice his arms were so long, they almost dragged onto the ground. No monster looked the same. The assortment was similar to the backyard: Some had long, spindly extremities coming off of deformed bodies. Some had horns, some tails, or forked tongues, some even looked as though their necks were broken and hanging to one side as they struggled to stay upright. Another couple dozen shadow people littered the street and front lawn of the house, their eyes lit by some dark force, like motionless fireflies. A few were even peering into the windows, like curious space aliens trying to find an abductee. One of them was on the porch right next to the door, and walked towards Scott. The rest saw Scott and lurched towards him with vigor. This time Scott was not keen on leaving the door open to take it all in. The door slammed, and the panic that Scott was feeling turned to sheer paralysis. Was this just another dream? Or rather, a nightmare?

"What do we do?" Andrea's descent into the first stages of madness was overcoming her ability to think rationally. She was looking to Scott to take the lead over this, but he was miles away, locked in a prison of his own fear and confusion. Both of them were no help to their son, who was terrified beyond anything a child should be able to withstand. Andrea shook Scott aggressively, her eyes flooded with tears. "Damn it, Scott, what are we going to do?!"

"Nothing." The calm, soothing voice behind them made the Dunnhill's jump with fright. The kind old face of Mr. Harris, dressed in a polo shirt and khaki slacks, beamed a huge grin at them from across the house, smack dab in the middle of the living room. The moment was so surreal that he seemed 100 feet away. "I'm afraid there's nothing left for you to do. It's time." He clasped his hands together, as if delivering bad news but enjoying it at the same time.

"Time for what? What is going on, and why are you in my house?!" Scott found what little courage he had to eliminate the bubble in his throat that was muting his speech. Call it genuine curiosity overcoming fear, or call it pure adrenaline. Scott had just enough in him to engage Mr. Harris.

"Three years is a long time. Too long, if you ask me. But the blood needed to age a little more. You've lasted a lot longer than any of the other families. But your time is up." Mr. Harris proudly beamed at them as they stood huddled together. "We're here for the boy."

"What? What are... What are you going to do?" Andrea tried very hard to speak as she fought back sobbing and heavy breathing.

"We're going to take turns raping and eating him on the dark altar." Mr. Harris' smile never left his face. "We need his blood."

It is believed, by this point, that Andrea began to disassociate with reality. That's when Mr. Harris, his grin dropping and his tone more serious, said the last thing he would ever say to the Dunnhill's.

"It's too late for the boy. But you can still save yourselves."

As Mr. Harris grinned again, his kind old eyes growing dark as he lowered his head, the lights dimmed out in the house and in the pitch black darkness, banging and shuffling filled the night. All around them. Stomping upstairs and in the attic assaulted their ears. What must have been hands and other appendages banged and slapped from inside the walls. The Dunhill's all reached towards each other in a vain attempt to hold on one last time. A low, slow screech, horrifying but not guttural or high pitched, emanated through the area around them in a ten foot radius. It sounded almost sad, as if dozens of damned souls were crying out for mercy."Ruuuuuuuuh!" It was almost deafening, and it only grew louder as it continued. Andrea clutched Jason tightly to her hip, and Scott held his family close.

Suddenly, the noise stopped, the lights came back on, and everything was silent. Mr. Harris was nowhere to be seen. Above them, a low voice spoke to them, as if from thin air. While they were able to understand it, it was not human, but rather sounded like something was trying to do it's best impression of a human voice.

"It's going to be a very long night."

Adrenochrome \ ə-ˈdrē-nō-ˌkrōm \ (n.) : a red-colored mixture of quinones derived from epinephrine by oxidation.

There is an increasingly popular belief among conspiracy theorists that the financial, political, and cultural elite all belong to a Satanic cult, and have been using their power and influence to insert more figures of power into society in an attempt at global domination. This could allegedly be achieved by manipulating currencies, creating laws, and conditioning the public through art and media. Many call this cabal of Satanists *The Illuminati*. Many more still refer to it simply as the *New World Order* (A term which is actually meant to describe the overall plan at global domination and not the clandestine group that allegedly perpetuates it).

For decades now, these conspiracies have tied this group to Satan via the use of the term "enlightened," the latin term for enlightened being *illustratum*. Lucifer (literally "The Light," with the latin term for illuminated being *illuminatum*) was able to tempt Eve into consuming the forbidden apple, a representation of knowledge. This is technically incorrect, as the tree which bore such fruit in the Bible was actually known as "The tree of the knowledge of good and evil," and many scholars debate whether the tree had a moral insinuation, or that the use of "good and evil" was an expression being conveyed by using a literary device known as a *merism*, which utilizes opposing concepts to paint a more generalized meaning. Thus, the use of *good and evil* is meant to mean *everything*, which in and of itself is quite Buddhist.

This whole idea, of course, comes off as overtly bogus to the average person.

While it can be darkly fun to speculate on why our favorite popstars insert Illuminati symbolism into their work, or use dark, pseudo-Satanic themes in their imagery, no known proof of this exists. Just like you can expect a Wall Street broker to embezzle money and devour the little guy, and just like you can expect a career politician to slip a controversial law into a bill, you can also expect that celebrity entertainers will use controversy to drum up attention, which will inevitably translate to money. But the terrifying part, the part that the average sane, rational person does not like to think about, is that all of this, while wholly unrealistic, is entirely within the realm of possibility.

An even more radical idea lies in the fringes of conspiracy theory circles. Like most Satanic cabals, there is an immense importance placed on ritual. Long ago, pagan and witchcraft rituals were characterized by animal or human sacrifice, consumption of blood or flesh, scrawling of runes and symbols, and crude altars made of natural elements such as stone, leaves, feathers, or branches. It was believed that consuming a living being as it screamed in fear and begged for its' life gave an otherworldly power to the consumer. The eaters of living flesh placed upon the altar experienced a journey into another realm, a shared realm, and upon returning would (allegedly) bring back an immense power that was capable of altering reality. As time went on, pagan beliefs faded away into the dusts of time and a more intellectual, scientific approach to this phenomenon warranted study.

And so there was. After World War II, German scientists who were studying the effects of ritualistic Satanic torture on their subjects were absorbed into the United States military in what is known as Operation Paperclip, and were tasked with continuing their research for the CIA to develop methods of mind control in what is known now as Project MK Ultra. This was an important moment for conspiracy theorists, who now had definitive proof of at least one of the many outlandish ideas they had devoted much of their time and degrading mental health into exploring. If this one was true, certainly other theories could be true as well. Through this research, it is said, there is a chemical that the body naturally creates in moments of intense fear and pain that travels from the brain and mixes into the muscles, tissue, and organs of the body. Further examination concluded that this chemical contained traces of an extremely potent neuronarcotic, and high ranking members of the United States Military called for further extensive studies into the effects of the chemical, and authorized human testing into its' effects. The officer in charge of this operation was Lt. Colonel Michael A. Aquino, a specialist in psychological warfare, a High Priest in the Church of Satan, and the eventual founder of the Temple of Set.

The chemical is known as adrenochrome.

So if the idea of widely circulated Satanic cults infiltrating our day to day lives and eating our children to get high and allegedly gain power is feasible, if not highly unlikely, how is it that nobody hears about it on the news, or sees any police reports in the local paper? How is it that adrenochrome is no longer listed as having any psychoactive properties after very limited testing in the early 1960's stated that it did? It could only make sense if Satanic cults existed not only in scattered local municipalities (a belief referred to as

Satanic Panic by news outlets in the 1980's), but had also infiltrated higher levels of government, the scientific community, law enforcement, and news media. In effect, it is only possible if they branched out and were secretly representing everything good and evil in the world.

Everything. Good and evil. Which in and of itself is quite Buddhist.

Of course, the irony of all of this was unknown to the Dunnhill's, who had a very long night ahead of them.

Andrea Dunnhill was almost comatose with fear. It was all so much at one time. But Scott didn't have time to understand this. He had to protect his family in any way that he could. The normal procedure, as he had played over and over in his head should there be any kind of intruder, was to lock the family in a room and call 9-1-1. But this was no home invasion. And he certainly wasn't going to go back outside. Which left just plain calling 9-1-1. Scott rushed around the living room looking for his phone. The couch sat pressed against the back door, and everything was eerily silent. Mr. Harris was nowhere to be seen. And Scott had a feeling that if he walked outside right now, his house would still be surrounded by monsters.

Monsters that were getting closer and closer to the house. Monsters that were already inside, waiting in the walls.

Andrea stood there, motionless. Scott bounded up to her. "Andrea, honey, I need to find my phone. Where is it?" Andrea just stared off into space, completely unable to process what was happening. "God damn it, Andrea, where is my fucking phone?!" Scott snapped his fingers aggressively in Andrea's face. He would have slapped her if he didn't suddenly realize that his son was standing right next to him. He looked over at Jason. "Son, help me look for my phone."

Just as soon as he asked, Scott looked at the kitchen breakfast bar that was adjoined to the living room and saw his phone, charging on the wall. Scott rushed over to it and turned it on. It buzzed and beeped it's normal introductory message before going to the loading screen, which Scott had zero patience for. At this point, Scott yearned for the old days when everybody had land line phones.

Scott dialed out to 9-1-1 and immediately there was loud banging, like the footsteps of a giant running at top speed directly above their heads. The footsteps rounded the corner in the hallways to the head of the stairs, and continuing their momentum, clomped downstairs like a horse and ran directly towards Andrea, who screamed at the top of her lungs and raised her hands in the air to protect herself. However, there was nothing there. No monster, no ghoul, no crazy neighbor. Just the loud, banging footsteps, which stopped as soon as they were within a foot away. Andrea crumpled to the ground and curled up into a ball, sobbing. Jason crouched down to protect her, and Scott finally got somebody on the phone.

"9-1-1, what's your emergency?" The caring voice on the other end of the phone was a welcome and inviting thing right now, but Scott was nearly paralyzed at this point. Finally gaining his composure after the phantom stomping, Scott quickly realized he would have to be vague, and leave out details if he wanted the police to show up. At this point, he was marred by both not knowing what to say, and being too confused and scared to form a cohesive thought process. "Yes, uh, my name is Scott Dunnhill, uh, there are people in my house, and, uh… They're banging on the walls, trying to, uh, intimidate us, and we're very scared, we really need the police out here, please! We need a lot of police!"

The operator maintained her composure. "Stay calm sir, we just need your address and then we can send help. What is your address?"

"312 Derby Lane," Scott responded.

The operator did not respond. Scott thought that maybe she was typing out an APB to send the force over. When she did finally speak again, Scott froze in terror, and the life force sank out of his body: "It's going to be a very long night, Mr. Dunnhill." And with that, she hung up.

The phone now silent in his ear, Scott trembled. He looked to his family, and dread overcame him. *We aren't going to make it out of here alive*, he thought. Jason looked up at Scott, possibly searching for a shred of hope, but found nothing. Scott, not wanting to let his son down, swiped through the contacts on his phone and found Martin and Linda's number.

The phone rang once and was picked up almost as if Martin was waiting for the call. "Hey there, Scott. What's going on?"

Scott looked around nervously, worried that another phantom would pound into the room. "Martin, I know it's late, but we're in a lot of trouble and we need some help."

"Well, what seems to be the problem?" Martin was his usual calm self, and it almost angered Scott at that moment.

"I don't think… Look, you wouldn't believe me if I told you. Just, can you…" Scott realized that calling the police from Martin and Linda's wasn't going to help. And it wasn't until that realization set in that he realized calling Martin was just a waste of time.

"Scott? What's the problem?" Martin asked.

"You already know what's going on, don't you?" All of Scott's weight sank to his feet.

"Of course. Chris called to Jason on that little radio of theirs. He had to be punished, unfortunately." Martin was very casual about all of it, much like Mr. Harris. "Scott? I want to hear you say it."

Scott didn't want to give him the satisfaction. What would happen if he didn't? Would they all come bursting in, one by one, and eat his family as he watched helplessly? Or would they devour him first, the last thing he saw being his family crying out in desperation and hopelessness as they were grabbed too? "But you already know. Why are you doing this?"

"Say it. I want to hear you say it." Martin's voice grew deeper, with an almost primal sexuality. "Say it!" He barked over the phone.

Scott closed his eyes tight, and swallowed his pride. "My house is surrounded by monsters and there's nobody coming to help us."

Martin chuckled lightly over the phone, not losing the darkly sexual hint in his voice. "Yes. And when you're hanging from the ceiling, hooks dug into your bones, your spine shattered, helpless to do anything, I'm going to cut a hole in your boy's stomach and fuck the wound. I'm going to drop my seed in his belly, and then I'm going to feast on his raw flesh, Scott. And he's going to beg for you to help him, and you won't be able to do anything but watch!" Martin hung up on Scott, who sank to the ground and cried.

Jason had never seen his dad cry. Even when he had bumped his head on the work table in the garage, or when Jason accidentally deleted an important project on Scott's computer when attempting to install a video game. But this was something completely different. Jason was torn between consoling his mother and trying to bring his father back to his feet and hopefully figure a way out of this. As he made his way across the now couchless living room, a small, vulnerable voice spoke from behind him.

"Jason?"

Jason turned to see the back of Chris, standing there in the middle of the living room. His head hung down low, and he was still in his plaid pajama pants and blue sleep shirt. "Chris? Oh my God, Chris, what's happening? What were you trying to tell me over the radio?" Scott looked up from his crumpled position on the floor, almost as catatonic as Andrea. Jason inched closer to Chris, who didn't move a muscle.

"I got in trouble, Jason. My mommy and daddy punished me." In that instance, two voices spoke out of Chris's mouth. One was Chris's, and the other was deep, ethereal, and scary. Jason stopped moving towards his friend. He had seen plenty of television, and always knew to be cautious in these situations. Chris removed his shirt and pajama pants, and was soon wearing only his underwear. Large welts and deep gashes, oozing with blood, covered his poor, tiny little body. "I'm in a lot of pain, Jason. I need your help. I need you to come to me. Please?"

Jason cried. He was so hopelessly out of his element that he couldn't help it. "I want to help you, Chris. I really do. But I can't."

"But I called you, Jason. I tried to help you. I got punished for it. Please, just take me away from all of this." Chris's voice still sounded like there was a second person inside of his mouth, speaking in unison with him. "I got in trouble for you, Jason." The other voice took over, and it was distorted from reality. "Come to me."

"No," said Jason.

Chris's head jerked back at a 90 degree bend, and a loud crack could be heard. As he struggled to maintain balance, the upper half of his body bent slowly towards Jason, more cracks and breaks echoing through the room. His ankles twisted backwards, so that his feet were now facing Jason, but his legs were still facing away. The upper half of Chris' body kept contorting towards Jason, completely perpendicular to the ground, until Jason found himself looking Chris in the face, his chin pointing upwards to the ceiling. Chris's eyes were now three times the size of human eyes, but still the same color as they always were. His mouth was now widened and elongated to cover almost the entire bottom of his face. Chris's left arm snapped backwards to point towards Jason.

"I've literally bent over backwards for you, you fucking prick, and all you can do is think of yourself?!" The little voice that was mimicking Chris had now taken over, and gotten louder and deeper to boot. "I can't wait for them to fuck you to death on the dark altar! Get over here!" Chris growled menacingly and hobbled at top speed towards Jason, who turned around sharply and ran for the stairs as fast as he could, screaming and crying at the top of his lungs. Scott, who was still on the floor, tried to reach out to stop Chris, but could not reach his ankle in time.

Jason scrambled up the stairs and felt like a hamster in a wheel. He knew, without even needing to think consciously about it, that he couldn't outrun Chris, or whatever this thing was that was using Chris. This thing that should not be. Jason would have to hide.

He reached the top of the stairs and turned a sharp left towards his bedroom. Chris leapt over the top four steps and growled in his ear as he gripped the shoulder of his pajamas. Jason wriggled free just as soon as he was grabbed and made it to the threshold of his bedroom. He tried to slam the door, but Chris' arm got through at the last minute. Jason kept slamming the door over and over on Chris' arm. He could see through the slit in the door. Chris was laughing, letting Jason slam the door on his arm intentionally. Slowly, Chris moved his arm out of the path of the door and backed away, smiling his demonic smile, shaking with silent laughter, and disappeared from sight.

Jason had seen plenty of horror movies. But at a time like this, fear can make even the most cautious of us do the most irrational things.

Jason slammed the door, locking it behind him, and scurried into the closet.

As Scott scrambled back up to his feet, Chris was clomping up the stairs towards his son. Scott wasn't sure if he could make it in time, but he had to try. He raced up the stairs as fast as he could, using his arms and legs like a dog to gain more speed. He lifted his head and saw Chris round a corner towards Jason's room, and heard a door slam. Maybe Jason got to his room in time. Maybe he shut the door right before Chris got to him. Scott would not be able to find out, unfortunately. The stairs rumbled under him, rippling fluidly, as if somebody on the other end had grabbed them and shaken them about like a rug.

Scott tumbled backwards down the stairs. He reached out for the railing but was not able to grab it in time. As he crashed head first to the hardwood floor of the living room, he felt blood stream down his face, and a throbbing pressure built up in his nose and forehead. Scott had only had one other head wound like this, when a log he was cutting off a tree on the side of the house fell and hit him. But this was worse. Jason was in trouble, and Scott was feeling more and more helpless by the minute.

"He's alone up there. In the dark." Andrea sat on the floor of the living room where the couch used to be, her legs splayed off to her left side, her right arm barely able to prop her up. Her face was

blank, her eyes wide open with trauma and fear. "He'll try to hide in the closet." Andrea turned her head sharply towards Scott and her eyes widened even further. "They'll pull him out. They'll pull our boy out by the legs, kicking and screaming."
Andrea began to sob. Scott grabbed a nearby chair and slammed it into the floor until one of the legs broke off. He took the broken leg in his hand like a club and ran to the stairs again. This time, nothing was going to stop him.

Andrea's lifeless gaze followed him, and her brow furrowed with mental anguish. Her voice rose to a shriek. "Kicking and screaming! Kicking and screaming! Kicking and Screaming!" She repeated this as Scott barreled up the stairs.

The stairs shook like a raging volcano. Scott used the railing to steady himself on the left, and his forearm kept him from falling over to his right side. As his forearm brushed against the wall of the upper section of the staircase, a hand, as if a part of the wall itself, grabbed him and tried to force him back down. He struggled to free his forearm from the powerful, monstrous grip, but discovered he was unable to move his left foot. Another hand, this one a part of the carpeting on the stairs, grabbed his entire leg from the calf to the ankle. Scott could feel himself dropping down slowly. A large slit appeared below him between two of the steps, which opened into a gaping hole, and as he sank further down, Scott knew the stairs had come to life, and were trying to devour him. Now waist deep in the staircase's newly formed mouth, he struggled to fight his way back to the stairs, and cried out to Andrea for help. As the stairs gnawed on his shoulders and neck, he looked back to his wife, who was now grinning ear to ear, rocking back and forth, and shuddering. And as he disappeared from sight, sliding down his staircase's gullet, his forearm wriggling in last ditch desperation to pull himself out, the last thing he could hear was her voice.

"Kicking and screaming! Kicking and screaming! Kicking and screaming!"

Jason closed the closet door behind him and fumbled around in the dark for another flashlight. He had no idea where the one by his bedside was, but he knew he had another in his toy chest. As he pulled toy after toy out and tossed them over his shoulder, he wondered what was happening to his parents at that moment. He wanted to run. Out of the house, down the street, into the next town, Hell, the next state even. But he knew he couldn't.

Jason found his flashlight. He was almost too scared to turn it on. The rationality settled back in, and he realized that, yes, he was indeed trapped. And hiding in a closet was not going to help him. Jason swallowed his fear and flicked the flashlight on. This one was brighter than the toy flashlight he used earlier when he saw the tree monster outside his window. He whipped the light around the closet, inspecting every corner, nook, and cranny. Nothing. Just a closet. Just a regular closet, with regular clothes, toys, and clutter. And no weapon. Nothing to protect him. Where was his dad? Why hadn't he come upstairs yet?

Four knocks disrupted his thought process. Four quiet, successive knocks that made him jump. As if whoever was knocking didn't want to disturb whatever was going on in the room. Was it his dad? Jason had seen plenty of movies. *Don't open the door.* Jason searched deep within him for his voice.

At first, the words didn't even come out. Jason realized he hadn't even been breathing since he got into the closet. "Who is it?" Finally, the words seeped out and were barely audible.

Silence. No response. Whatever was on the other side of the door didn't want Jason to know what it was. Four more knocks cut into the quiet solitude of the closet. "I'm not going to answer until I know who's knocking." More silence. Anxiety fell over Jason, and he started breathing heavier, almost in a panic. Then, a soft, calm voice came through on the other side, muffled by the wood.

"It's Mr. Maxwell, Jason. Come on out of the closet." Chris's dad? What was he doing here? Did he get through the wall of monsters outside?

"Where's my dad?" Asked Jason.

"He's fine, son. He's downstairs, waiting for you right now. He's hurt, though. We need you to come downstairs. We're going to get you guys out of here." Mr. Maxwell didn't raise his voice. Not like he did on the phone with Jason's dad. Was there something that overtook him too? Was this the real Mr. Maxwell?

"I heard you on the phone with my dad earlier." Jason didn't know what to do. The area he was trapped in went from the house to this little four foot space. The world was closing in on him, and he was in danger of being consumed by it's darkness.

"That wasn't me, Jason. I swear. Something is going on. I don't know what yet. But the same thing happened to Chris." Said Mr. Maxwell.

"Where is Chris?" Asked Jason.

"He's at home. He's fine. Come downstairs." Mr. Maxwell's tone was beginning to tighten.

Jason pondered the possibility that this was all an elaborate ruse. He decided he didn't want to risk anything. "No."

"I could just open the door and grab you. Take you downstairs myself." Mr. Maxwell had a point. "Or, you can just come out of there. It's your choice."

Jason grew slightly more defiant. "I'm not coming out of here until my dad says so." Jason waited with full paralysis for Mr. Maxwell to open the door and drag him out.

Silence. Jason couldn't even hear Mr. Maxwell breathing. Was he even standing outside the door? After a moment, his voice came softly through the door again. "That's fine. But you should have chosen a better hiding spot, Jason. Certainly not the closet. That's where the Tarantula Man lives."

Perhaps Mr. Maxwell was there to serve as a distraction. Perhaps he was some kind of conjurer of monsters and demonry. Regardless of what his true purpose was, he kept Jason fixated on the door, and not the ceiling above him. So when the long, spindly, hooked legs skittered onto Jason's head, Jason had nothing that could prepare him for it. Perhaps Mr. Maxwell's plan all along was just to get Jason out of the closet. If that was the plan, then it worked all too perfectly.

A dull, raspy, fast paced clicking sound emanated above Jason's head and more spider legs caressed him. His shoulders, arms, and legs now had the soft, uncomfortable feeling of large spiders skittering about, and Jason, acting purely on survival instinct, burst out of the closet. He ran out into his bedroom, and panicked when he realized there was nowhere else to go. The window was guarded by the tree monster, Chris was possibly still outside the door, and as he turned around, the six armed man in the black suit and the tarantula legs for fingers that he saw outside earlier leapt out of the closet and wrapped his limbs around Jason's body.

He wasn't heavy. At least, not as heavy as he looked. While he was tall, Jason discovered, he was also very spindly. His arms and legs couldn't have been thicker than a broom handle. Each limb, it seemed, was segmented, so that it could wrap itself perfectly around Jason's body. Jason tried to run away, as much as he could move his legs at least. He was so overcome with panic that he accidentally slammed into a wall in his bedroom. The Tarantula Man let out a loud, guttural cry of pain as a snapping sound cracked through the room. He dropped off of Jason's body, and crumpled to the floor, his limbs curling up into his torso like a spider that had just been sprayed with bug killer.

Before Jason could even think, a long arm with long, pointed fingers grabbed his leg and pulled him down to the floor. He reached out for whatever he could but found nothing, and looked down at his ankle to see glowing red eyes underneath the bed. He struggled to prevent the monster from pulling him under, and started kicking the arm. "Don't try to fight me, little boy! Come under the bed! I have candy!" Maniacal laughter emanated from underneath the bed, and Jason finally wriggled free of the monster's grip. Jason realized the only way to get out would be the bedroom door. He quickly looked around for a weapon and found his baseball bat against the dresser.

Jason hurried cautiously out of his bedroom, clutching the bat close to his body, ready to swing at anything that moved. The house was eerily silent. In a way, Jason relished this moment. Silence meant nothing was happening. If Jason called out to his parents, what would spring out and ensnare him next? Once again, his fear battling his rationality, Jason found his voice again. "Dad? Mom?"

Silence. As he approached the stairs, the door to his parent's bedroom flew open and a hulking beast roared out towards him, arms stretched upwards. It had a pale red skin and long, dark horns that curled downward to it's cheeks. It's tongue dragged below it's chin, slobbering drool, and it's massive red eyes and long, hooked teeth bared down upon Jason. As it ran for him, the upstairs hallway distorted outward, bulging larger, as if to accommodate the seven foot tall monster, and it banged the palms of it's hands loudly against the walls. It's claws could have snatched Jason with ease. Whether he knew attacking the creature would be meaningless or whether he was just too scared to do anything else, Jason dropped the bat and ran off towards the stairs, screaming. "Mom! Mom! Help!" Jason flew down the stairs, bounding four to five steps at a time.

Curiously, as Jason reached the bottom of the stairs, he looked around and saw… Nothing. Absolutely nothing. Just silence again. Was the house toying with him? His heart was beating in his chest faster than a stock car engine, and he twirled about in place for a moment, paranoid and delusional. He could swear he heard a noise over there, or a bump over here. But all he saw was his mother, crumpled on the floor, helpless. Just staring. Staring at the back door. "Mom!" He rushed to her side and knelt down to get her attention. But Andrea was miles away.

Accounts of Andrea Dunnhill's experiences during the long night at 312 Derby Lane were harder to come by during the research. Given the nature of her situation, some of these accounts come from third parties whose interactions with her were questionable, or people who had met her in passing. Most of what we know comes from self-correspondence, which gained us valuable insight until the trail went cold. Much of it is incoherent, and certain educated guesses had to be made to piece things together. It was the most exhaustive portion of the study, and thus certain liberties must be taken to fill in the holes of her story. Rest assured, these liberties do not come lightly. Everything that Andrea did that was separate from any witnesses was thoroughly poured over and meticulously analyzed.

Andrea's mental state had fractured in two at this point. Already having been bombarded with an array of emotions from the afternoon, stretching into the evening, there was no time for her to process or calm down. When she saw monsters for the first time, it is believed that she slipped into a dissociative mental state. That is to say, she separated the reality of what she was experiencing with the reality she wished to be experiencing, and was caught in a sort of mental limbo, her mind completely pliable.

So when Jason came to his mother's side to comfort her, the woman he had known his whole life had changed. In his own fragile, delicate mental state, Jason did not know what to do to snap his mother back to reality. How could he? He was merely a ten year old boy and was scared, lost and confused. His father was nowhere to be found, and only a short time ago, he was hiding in his closet, afraid of the monsters.

Jason could not have possibly known that the stairs had swallowed his father. He could not possibly have known anything that was happening downstairs while he was hiding.

That his mother was talking to the neighbors.

As Andrea watched her husband disappear into the stairs, it had finally happened. She had snapped. Her words trailed off from a shriek to a mere whisper. "Kicking... And screaming... Kicking... And screaming..." She did not move for what seemed like hours, but were actually mere minutes. She was so blank, she did not notice Linda, Katie, Donna, or Bridgette walk into the living room, move the couch back to it's rightful place, and sit down for drinks.

"I keep telling you, the curtains in here are so drab. We can't even see the shadows outside."

Bridgette Monroe waxed on about the décor in this Satanic hell hole that was 312 Derby Lane. "Hopefully, the next couple that moves in will have some brighter taste."

"And hopefully they'll be more open minded about their interior decorating!" Donna Harris let out a loud, screeching cackle, an ungodly sound that could not possibly have come from the mouth of a human being. Her jaw elongated 4 inches downward as she did, and the other three women joined her.

"Donna, you're terrible!" Said Katie Branford jokingly. "I just want the next family to bring us a girl. I still feel an emptiness inside of me after our biological daughter died. She wasn't filling enough."

Linda chimed in. "You didn't let her taste build up. Of course the meat was sour. And her blood had no potency. We barely stayed afloat that year."

Katie looked to Andrea. "I blame the housing market. We couldn't even get this place sold. It was a miracle when you and Scott moved in. We didn't want to do it, honestly. Our daughter, I mean. We sort of hoped she would take to it, become one of us. Our little Hannah." Katie Branford crossed her legs as she detailed why she had sacrificed her and Robert's only child. "Jessica did, of course, but Hannah struggled with it. She was horrified the first time we brought her downstairs. Poor thing ran away, crying. We had to chase her down the street and bash her little head into the curb. She wasn't ready. Not like Jason."

"Oh, he's such a lively young man, isn't he?" Donna spoke up. "I'm an older lady, Andrea, and I was so happy when you moved in and brought us a boy. There's so much more life and vigor in them!" Donna cackled again, and the collective cackling of the four women almost cracked the windows.

Bridgette turned her gaze towards Andrea, who sat motionless on the floor, barely noticing the conversation going on in front of her. "Andrea, honey, I forgive you for your outburst this morning." She placed her hand on Andrea's shoulder. "I may have overreacted just a tad, but it's because I just value our friendship so much. Don't you value my friendship, Andrea?" Andrea nodded her head and placed her hand over Bridgette's. "That's good. Come, get up off the floor and have a seat. Ooh, this couch is comfy. Isn't it girls?" Bridgette slowly helped Andrea to her feet as the other three women nodded their heads in agreement.

Andrea sat down on the couch. "It's like a cloud, isn't it?" Said Bridgette. And she was right. Andrea at once felt peaceful and relaxed. A small, slight smile crept up the right side of her face, her eyes still bleary with tears. "Just makes you want to sit and disappear into this couch, doesn't it? All your problems, just melting away." Andrea nodded in agreement, her smile gaining a little bit more real estate of her face. She looked at Bridgette, and then the other women, her smile increasing in size. Tears streamed down her cheek as she engaged in the rapturous company of her friends. Her friends, from whom she was not receiving hatred and spite, but acceptance and love.

"Andrea, honey? The dark one won't be appeased unless we have Jason. He'll punish all of us if you don't give him over. He'll punish you, too." Andrea's smile faded away as Linda spoke. "You've never seen the master punish us. We've all been punished at some point in time or another." The other women nodded solemnly. "He'll lash your wrists to the wall, and those monsters out there will take turns raping you." Andrea's eyes welled with tears again, her smile fell right off her face, and her lips trembled in fear. A low moan of pain and terror escaped her mouth, and she looked helplessly to her friends. "They'll tear your clothes off in front of Jason. He'll be forced to watch as they peel off your skin. You don't want that, do you?" Andrea shook her head meekly, and couldn't quite eek out the word no, letting only her lips make the motion.

"We just want the boy. Then you and Scott can go, far away from here. Or you can stay with us, and have power. Real, true power." Katie's reassuring voice was soothing, and brought Andrea back into her pillowy mental nirvana. "You can finally be happy, Andrea."

"Happy…" Andrea whispered. The very word sent blissful delight throughout her whole body, and she smiled. The women stood her back up to her feet, and moved the couch back to the door it was barricading.

"Jason is coming down the stairs soon, Andrea. He's fine. Everything is fine. We just need you to bring him to us." Bridgette placed her hand on Andrea's shoulder again. Pure, unadulterated exaltation warmed the air around her at Bridgette's favorable reception.

"But what will happen to Jason?" Andrea hesitated, looking around her. The house didn't seem so bright anymore, the world didn't seem as safe. "What will you do to my son?"

"You don't need to worry about that anymore, Andrea. You just need to bring Jason to us. And then you'll finally be happy." Andrea stopped and thought about everything that was being said. She smiled again, and looked to her friends. The four women left her in the living room, and as she sank back down to the floor, euphoria overcame her.

"I'll finally be happy."

Scott fell for what seemed like an eternity.

When he did finally land, the ground was soft, almost mushy, however the impact sent a sharp pain up his left leg. Scott was fairly certain it was broken, however eventual medical testing indicated it was a hairline fracture. Even still, Scott had great difficulty rising to his feet, and even greater difficulty moving around with speed. A light flickered in the distance, and as his eyes adjusted to the darkness, he could tell that he was in some kind of cave system. Pemberton was roughly twenty or so miles from the Rockford Cavern system. But what was the likelihood that the entire system ran underneath his house?

Scott didn't have time for trivial matters. He had to get to his son. If Jason was even still alive. *Oh God, no.* With hope fading fast, Scott's will to continue dwindled like a flame on a spent candle. He tore off the sleeves of his night shirt and used the broken chair leg to fashion a crude splint, then set out to follow the barely flickering light at the end of the caves tunnel. Water dripped all around him, echoing through the corridor of rock and moss, making it difficult to hear much else.

Something behind him startled him enough to seek a hiding place. A tall, lanky creature waddled towards him, it's arms dragging along the ground. Scott took cover behind a large rock and peered just past it to see what was hobbling past. It had long, brittle strands of hair, and in the dark it appeared to have gray skin and a large nose and an extreme underbite. Behind it, a man who looked severely beaten was being dragged, a streak of blood visibly staining the ground as he slid past. The monster stopped right in front of the rock that Scott was hiding behind, and looked around.

Scott hoped to God that this thing couldn't smell him, or hear him. Scott held his breath as much as he could, but his lungs were filled with dust and still weak from the fall. Scott let a moment pass before trying to peer over the rock. The creature had already passed, and it's lurking form sashayed it's way towards the light. Scott dreaded the thought of having to follow that thing. But even more so, Scott dreaded what it was that thing was moving towards.

Scott limped towards the light at the end of the tunnel. He stopped dead in his tracks when a whisper reached out for him in the darkness. He could feel it's presence, but even in the dim light, he couldn't see anything. "Keep moving forward, Scott." It sounded like the voice from before, the one in the living room that seemed to come from nowhere. The voice that seemed to start all of this.

"Who is that? Who's talking to me?" Scott kept his voice low enough to not let it echo down into the tunnel.

"You're almost there. You're almost at the dark altar, Scott. And when you get there, you'll watch. You'll see all of it. It will last for hours. And it will be beautiful." The voice faded way. "It's going to be a long night."

Scott continued towards the dark altar. Whose voice was that? One of his neighbors? A demon? It didn't matter. A twinge of hope reentered Scott, as he remembered what they said. They were going to place Jason upon the dark altar. They would rape and eat him. If there was even a tiny chance that Scott could free Jason and get his family to safety, then he had to take it.

Scott finally closed in on the end of the tunnel. He heard drumming, chanting, and haunting screams. As he came to the end of his long walk, the tunnel opened up into a massive cavern roughly the size of a football field. Long wooden pikes protruded from the ground around the edges of the cavern, with people crucified to them. Slender, clawed monsters with long snouts and sharp teeth crawled up the pikes toward their prey, and devoured them slowly, starting at the feet.

Horrified, Scott tried to look away, but everywhere he set his eyes he saw something worse. A torture device had a man suspended with chained hooks, his belly facing the ground. He was cut open at the stomach, and impish monsters held bright fiery torches up to this open intestines, laughing in manic delight. As he screamed, he looked down and cried at the corpse of a child, who could be no older than Jason. People in robes surrounded the lifeless child, his eyes still wide open in shock, and tore off bits of flesh, popping them in their mouths like it was a buffet. Ten feet away, two behemoth monsters held a naked woman's arms as she struggled to escape their grip, crying and screaming for mercy towards the child being devoured.

Scott tried to close his eyes, but he was dizzy with nausea. The room was spinning, and when he tried to move his gaze to something less disturbing, his eyes finally caught the middle of the cavern. Scott couldn't believe it wasn't the first thing he noticed. A large slab of stone, different from the rest of the rock in the cavern. Satanic markings were scrawled on the stone, possibly in blood, circling the entire thing. It must have been fifty feet across. Branches, mud, dead leaves, bones, and rock formed a monument in the center, a tower scaling one hundred feet high. And at the foot of the monument was a bed of stone, carved perfectly into a block, with a recessed bit that formed what looked almost like a bed. A blanket of leaves lay in the recessed divot, and candles burned brightly all around.

This must be it. Thought Scott. *The dark altar.*

He looked around again, and remembered the other sound he heard in his living room. The one that sounded like the souls of the damned crying out in pain. Suffering needlessly. They were all around him. And at that moment, Scott knew that Hell was a real place, it was on Earth, and that he was currently inside of it.

Jason gently shook his mother's shoulder. "Mom? Mom, are you okay?" He looked around, certain something else would creep up or jump down on him. The living room was silent. Motionless. Just like his mother.

Andrea slowly turned her head towards him. She spoke slowly, almost sedated. "I'm fine, son. I'm fine. Everything is fine."

Jason didn't know what to do, but he was pretty sure his mother was not doing well, and he was definitely sure that nothing was fine. "Mom, where's dad?" Jason feared the worst. That his father had made his way upstairs and had been eaten, or killed by one of the neighbors.

"He went to go get help, sweetie. Everything is fine." A small smile appeared at the corner of her mouth and she put her arms around her son. She placed her face right next to his ear and whispered. "This is just a dream. A scary dream. And to wake up from a dream, you have to get to the scariest part. When you're at your most frightened… That's when you'll finally wake up." She leaned back slightly, her hands clutching Jason's face in a motherly, nurturing way. "We're going to wake up very soon."

Jason just stared at his mother. His own mental state was breaking, and he wanted to believe her so badly. He slowly allowed himself to embrace the lie, and as his mother pulled him in closely, he nestled his face in her chest, feeling safe for the first time all night.

"It's time." A small, sweet voice interrupted their moment. Jason looked to his right and saw Jessica standing in the living room. "Are you coming willingly, or do we have to bring the monsters in?"

Andrea smiled, her eyes puffy from crying so hard. "He's coming willingly. He's ready to end this." Jessica turned and walked toward the front of the house. Andrea stood and held her hand out for Jason, who took it. They followed Jessica to the entrance hearth, where the little coat closet that is barely ever used faced them ominously. Jessica opened the door, and stepped inside, only to press a button hidden away in the wall. The wall slid open, and Jessica walked through.

Little Jessica was the subject of much debate within the department. It was suggested that she was the daughter of another family who had the misfortune of signing the lease for 312 Derby Lane. That she was either raised by the Branford's as a baby, or that she surrendered herself to them in order to escape a much worse fate. The closest thing anybody could find to an alternative theory was a little girl named Patricia Hartley who was left at an orphanage at the age of two. Over the years, the Hillwood Center for Orphaned Children had experienced multiple fatalities, all accidents, involving other children. Several administrators allegedly noticed a pattern; that the victims all had recent negative interactions with Patricia, but before any investigation could be executed, Hillwood burned down, along with every child, worker, and document. Whether or not the Branford's adopted Patricia Hartley, and if Patricia Hartley died in the fire, is not a matter of record, and is merely a speculation.

      Jessica led them down a long, winding set of stairs that was carved into solid rock. Clearly, this had been here for a long time. Jason looked at the back of his friend's head. Even without seeing her face, she felt cold, distant, and soulless. He remembered the time in the forest. When she tried to get him and Chris to eat the dead squirrel. Jason wondered if that, too, was a dream. If all of this wasn't just some big dream, and that he had been asleep all his life.

      They came to a large opening in the narrow, descending corridor of stairs, about ten feet wide. Drums, screams, chants, and crackling fire filled the air, along with hissing, roars, and laughter. From out of nowhere, a child ran up the stairs from the opening, and stopped short of Jessica. Fear was stuck on the child's face, and Jason recognized him as a boy from school named Max. Before Jason could process what was going on, Jessica reached forward, grabbed Max's arm, and ripped it clean off of his torso. Max screamed out, blood spurting all over the stairs. Jessica grabbed him by the back of his head, lifted him off the ground, and slammed his face into the stone floor at the foot of the stairs.

They aren't supposed to run off like that." Said Jessica. "Some of the businessmen visiting from The Midwest were supposed to make him have sex with a headless body before passing him around. Too bad." She held the arm out to Andrea. "You need to eat his flesh." Andrea reached forward, her eyes glazed over hypnotically, and took the arm from Jessica. Jason looked down in horror as Max's lifeless body laid out in a pool of blood. *When will the nightmare end?* He thought. *When will I wake up?* He looked to his mother, who was eyeing the arm intensely.

Andrea hesitated at first. Perhaps she wasn't so sure if she should do it, like there was some kind of moral qualm deeply ingrained in her. Perhaps seeing the child being slaughtered in front of her slightly snapped her back to reality, if only for a moment. But that moment was fleeting. "Eat it." Urged Jessica. "Eat it, and you will visit the other side. And when you come back, you will bring power with you." Andrea wanted to finally be happy, and she was ready. Ready to wake up. She dug into the flesh and took a giant bite, making sure to slurp up as much blood as she could. It dribbled down her chin like an infant eating baby food for the first time. She closed her eyes to savor every bite, and the soft, salty child meat made her taste buds explode with new flavors. And in this moment, Jason realized this could not possibly be a dream. The lie was bogus, and the illusion began melting away. He started to go back up the stairs, when Andrea grabbed his arm. Her pupils were dilated, her nostrils flared, and sweat poured down her face. She was high on adrenachrome, and she liked it. As she held him from escaping, her strength severely heightened, she bent down and got face to face with her son. Her vocal cords, possibly from the effects of the adrenachrome, swelled to make her voice deeper.

"It's time for you to wake up!"

Scott didn't have time to think this over.

As he scanned the horrors of the dark altar, hoping to find some shred of proof that Jason was there and praying it wasn't too late, Scott also tried to plot out an escape route. After all, he had been swallowed into the depths, with no method of going back the way he came. As he ducked down behind some rocks at the threshold of the cavern, he tried to find other places to hide in the chamber, so he was not seen when he inevitably had to descend the massive stone steps leading to the chamber floor. The monsters were the primary concern, of course, but another factor occurred to him: He could not let any of the victims see him, or they may cry out for help and give away his position.

As Scott studied the floor plan of the chamber, a scream billowed out from the right. At the far end of the chamber, another set of stone stairs led down to the chamber floor. Given that the light was so dim and the other side must have been at least 150 feet away, Scott couldn't make out the figures coming down the stairs. All he could see was a child, struggling with an adult, trying to free itself. Scott knew in his heart that it must be Jason. And so, he made his way slowly down the stairs to the killing floor, making sure not to attract too much attention. Any actions had to be deliberate and silent.

As Scott touched the ground floor, something peculiar happened. The people who hung from the pikes and chains all looked out toward the right side of the chamber, and the monsters that were devouring or torturing them took notice and slowly crept away. Scott had a window of opportunity to speed up a bit, and made his way toward the dark altar.

More monsters and even some people in dark robes walked up behind Scott, who ducked into a tent set up next to a stone slab table with crude, sharp tools laid out upon it, soaked in blood. Scott recalled a time in college when he and some friends attended a stock car racing event for the weekend. Thousands of people showed up, parked their vehicles on the lawn next to the massive stadium, and set up tents, beer pong tables, put out blankets and grills. This was like tailgating for Satanists.

Scott watched from behind the tent's flap and saw several of the monsters from outside of his house walking by, accompanied by a handful of robed people. One of the people in the robes spoke. "It's about time, sure, but I still think we should guard the house."

Another spoke. "All are required to be present when the Elder's perform their sacrificial rites."

"Don't tell me traditions and protocols, Janice, I'm well aware of how things are done. But not everybody is accounted for, and…" The voices trailed off as they walked away. Scott's hopes rose again. *They must be talking about Jason.* A hand wrapped around Scott's shoulder and yanked him backwards, sending him crashing to the floor. Scott couldn't help but make a startled noise, and turned to see a woman, half of her body missing, the other half rotting so badly it appeared that she was melting into the makeshift bed of leaves and twigs. Scott had heard about a Fort Dalton woman who had neglected her sick mother so badly that her appendages were stuck to the bed, sticky and slimy. How long had this woman been here?

"Did you escape? Did you find a way out? Tell my family what happened… And please, kill me… I can't bear it any longer." The woman pointed to a bloody, ceremonial knife on a table beside the crude bed. Scott grabbed it and held it over the woman. Perhaps it was instinct kicking in, the same instinct that led him to this point safely. Perhaps, with adrenaline rushing through his body, his senses had been heightened. Whatever it was, Scott turned around with lightning quick speed and stabbed a hooded figure who had just entered the tent behind him.

Blood spurted outwards from the wound, splattering Scott with hot red liquid. The man in the robe looked up, but Scott did not recognize him. He reached out and placed his hands on Scott's shoulders, attempting to support himself from falling over, but it all came around just the same. The man collapsed at Scott's feet and bled out on the cold ground. Scott turned around and faced the woman again. She stared up at him, but didn't say a word. When she closed her eyes, Scott slit her throat, ending her miserable life. He thought briefly about who she might have been, where she came from, and how she got here. Was she happy? Did she know any of these freaks, or did she just get picked up off the street one night? Scott snapped back to attention quickly and remembered he had to save his family.

Scott realized he would have to blend in to get a close enough look at what was going on, so he stripped the dead Satanist of his robes and put them on. The hood drooped over his face, and the knife was hidden in one of his sleeves, Scott exited the tent and transitioned into the line of monsters and men.

As they all sauntered towards the middle of the cavern, Scott could hear the screams and pleas of those above him. He wanted to help them all. He wanted to cut them all down and escape. But in a moment like this, your priorities take precedence. Scott had to be selfish in this instance. He lifted his head up just enough to see the dark altar, hidden only behind the heads and bodies in front of him. He tried to maneuver himself to see past those who stood in front of him, but did not want to risk being conspicuous.

As they approached the dark altar, everybody, from monster to human, found a place to gather around for a good view. Scott took this opportunity to move around a bit and get a better angle. So far, nobody was on the altar, save for a small group of people in robes. He immediately recognized them as his neighbors. *Were they the Elders?* Scott refocused and looked around. Everybody was lined up on two sides, facing each other, with about ten feet of space in between. Even though everybody was shoulder to shoulder, Scott could see through to the other end. And when he turned his attention to what everybody else was looking at, he saw a gigantic monster that walked on what looked like four human legs. A long, hooked snout with gnarled teeth and greasy black hair punctuated the glowing red eyes. Sweat dripped from the pores of it's grey/black skin, and it's arms were bulky, like a body builders. Instead of a torso, the abomination had an open chest cavity, and it's ribs acted as bars. It was a living cage, this creature, and locked away being walked to his death was Jason.

Scott fully intended on following the cage to the dark altar. Maybe he could intercept Jason and just run off before they caught him. Maybe he could grab another weapon, or even create a distraction and sneak Jason away. But all of that came to a halt when Scott saw something that both warmed his soul and froze his blood: The back of Andrea's head, directly in front of him. He wouldn't miss that wavy brown hair anywhere. But what was she doing just standing there? Was she also trying to free Jason? Wasn't she worried about getting caught? As if she could hear his thoughts, Andrea slowly turned her head around and looked Scott directly in the eye. "Oh, good. You're here." Andrea smiled at her husband.

"What are you doing here? You're going to get us killed." Whispered Scott.

"They're going to the other realm. Our boy is the doorway." Andrea's pupils were fully dilated, making her eyes look black. She pointed towards the dark altar and turned her head again to look at it.

"I've been there, Scott. I came back out, and..." She turned and faced him again. "I'm reborn, Scott. And... and it feels so good." Andrea was overcome with emotion and wept. She turned and embraced her husband. "I've never felt so alive, Scott. And you can feel this way, too." Scott looked over her shoulder at the cage monster, who was stopped before the dark altar. As Jason was being dragged from the cage kicking and screaming by the Elders, the crowd started chanting.

"Ha ha ha ha. Ha ha ha ha. Ha ha ha ha. Ha ha ha ha."

Andrea, as if switching to another channel, stepped away from Scott, turned, and chanted with the rest of the crowd. Scott felt hopeless, and panicked. Seeing Jason being placed upon the altar and having his clothes removed with a knife, Scott once again went into full on survival mode. He searched his surroundings, hoping to find any way possible to create chaos. He looked to the tents, then the pikes, then to something he hadn't even noticed before. Hanging by their feet from the cavern's roof just above Scott's head were charred, smoldering bodies, and below them at ground level, more bodies, bound with what looked like some kind of sticky, thick chemical that glistened in the torchlight. Scott looked at the area next to the corpses and saw barrels, bubbling and noxious. He slunk behind the crowd and grabbed a torch from one of the tents, and ran to the barrel, kicking it over and hoping to God his plan would work.

As the slime oozed amongst the feet and robes of the Satanic crowd, Scott threw the torch on the liquid, and it ignited, burning brightly. As it engulfed the crowd, several monsters lit up in flames, screaming, roaring, and screeching. It wasn't going to affect a lot of area, but it was just enough to get everybody's attention. *This is it. This is my chance.* Scott snuck around towards the dark altar, making sure to move amongst the tents and not be seen. As the crowd moved away from the altar and towards the fiery chaos and screaming, and the Elders' attention was placed on the anarchy happening amongst their subjects, Scott carefully ascended the steps of the altar, grabbed Jason, and carried him over his shoulder.

Scott made his way back down the steps, and into the small city of tents that made up the majority of the cavern. He held his son for one brief moment, just so he could look into his eyes and let him know that his father had come to rescue him. "Jason, it's me. It's dad. I'm going to take you away from here." Patches of Jason's hair had turned white, and he appeared half comatose. Scott didn't have time to coax a conversation out of his son. He picked him back up and continued to slink through the tents. He looked back with enough time to see that the Elders had turned around and noticed that Jason was gone.

"The boy is missing! He can't escape! Anybody who lets him will be punished severely! Find him!" Mr. Harris screamed at the top of his lungs. His voice boomed supernaturally across the expanse of the cavern, and when he spoke, every living thing scrambled around like ants after their pile has been stepped on. Scott knew he had to hurry out, and hiding in the tents wasn't going to work. So he continued to sneak his way through the paths.

Having studied the area, Scott knew where the exit point would be. Jason was brought in through a set of stairs about 100 feet away from the dark altar. Scott was now 50 feet away from those stairs. *Half way there.* Scott could hear footsteps coming around the corner of one of the corridor of tents, so he pushed Jason into the nearest tent and opened the flap, pretending to search the area and hoping they wouldn't notice. When the Satanists passed, Scott grabbed Jason again, and ran behind the cover of another section of tents as the tree monster made it's way above the human eyeline, searching from its' much higher vantage point. The tree monster began picking the tents up in it's large hands, piercing anything that existed inside with it's sharp, spindly fingers.

Scott moved into what he assumed was the tree monsters' blind spot and continued towards the exit. There were more people and creatures near the exit than anywhere else, and Scott had to think very quickly. He placed Jason down on the ground, climbed up onto a stone slab next to a tent, and pointed away from the staircase. "Over there! He's hiding among the rocks over there!" Immediately, the monsters rushed over to the area Scott pointed at, their snarls and roars and growls shaking the entire cavernous chamber. With the exit cleared, Scott picked Jason up and raced towards the stairs, almost tripping over the body of a small boy with one arm, laying in a puddle of blood. Scott kept moving as fast as he could, without looking back.

He didn't see Andrea, walking among the chaos, tracking his movements. Her eyes furrowed, and when she reached the foot of the stairs, she bent over, ripped poor Max's head off of his body, and ate his face.

Scott knew he wasn't in the clear yet. They were bound to send more of those fiends upstairs to search the house. There had to be other forces at play here, watching the streets. If the cops were in on it, maybe other people were too. No, they would only be safe when they were as far away from Pemberton as possible.

Scott made his way to the top of the stairs, but found a dead end. *A door,* he thought. *There must be a door.* He remembered being eaten by the floor. *Please, let there be a door.* He banged on the rocky wall at the head of the staircase, then set Jason down and started feeling around the area. In a matter of seconds, his hand rubbed up against a piece of rock that jutted out from the wall, and the hidden door slid open. Jason was still not responsive when Scott picked him up again. He went through the door and found himself in the hall closet. *The car keys.* Scott needed the keys, and his wallet, and his phone. Nothing else mattered.

He placed Jason down on the couch and went to the kitchen counter where he kept his keys in a bowl. His wallet, however, was upstairs. Not wanting to have a repeat of being eaten alive by his own floor, Scott decided the wallet was not that important. He turned to go back to the couch and check on Jason. But all he saw was Andrea, standing in the middle of the room, with her arms around Jason, who was also facing forward.

"What do you think you're doing, Scott?" Asked Andrea. Her eyes were cold and black.

"Andrea… We need to get out of here. All of us, okay? We're a family, and we need to protect our son." Scott did not know if pleading with his wife would be effective at this point. Something had happened, and she wasn't right in the head. Scott was worried she may never be again.

Tears strolled down Andrea's cheeks. Her tired eyes drooped, and her lip curled and quivered. "I have worked so hard, Scott… So damn hard." She took a step backwards with Jason. Scott moved a step forward to close the distance a little bit.

"What are you going to do? Where are you going with our son?!" Scott was frustrated. He didn't want to rush Andrea, or physically attack her, and he certainly didn't want her to take Jason back down there. She panicked, picked Jason up, and started to back herself towards the closet. Scott moved forward slowly with every step she took.

"I am going back down there, Scott, and I am going to end this all right now! I am going to save us. Don't you see?" Andrea's tears continued to stream down her face.

"What the Hell is the matter with you?! That's your son! You can't do this to your own son!" Scott tried to move closer to grab Jason, but Andrea dropped him and grabbed Scott by the throat. Scott struggled to free himself, but her grip was just too tight.

Her voice was deep again, as the adrenochrome was slowly seeping it's way back into her. "Do you have any idea what it's like? The power? I've transcended space and time. I've traveled to other realms, seen things I never thought were possible. I can do anything. I can answer all of life's questions, I just need more!" Andrea threw Scott to the ground, and grabbed Jason by the arm. She dragged him towards the closet again. "And you're not going to stop me."

Scott had a very important decision to make at this particular point, and he made it very easily. He pulled out the knife he had been hiding in his robes, stood up, and slammed the edge of the blade as hard as he could into Andrea's back. She flailed, writhed, and tried to reach back to pull it out. Scott grabbed Jason, picked him up, and was about to run outside to the car when he looked at the closet door. *They'll be here any moment*, he thought. *It's time to burn this mother fucker down to the ground.*

Scott ran to the fireplace and grabbed one of the starter logs that they kept next to it. On the mantle was a grill lighter, one of those long ones with the flexible nozzle. He lit the log and threw it into the closet. It burned rather fast, and the flames rose high enough to light the coats and scarves that hung there. Scott hoped that would be enough to go on, and he grabbed Jason and ran out the front door. Immediately, monsters began pouring into the house through the back door. Andrea pulled the knife out of her back and turned to face Scott. Perhaps it was the knife in her hand and the perceived threat it brought. Perhaps it was Mr. Harris' promise that anybody who let the boy go free would be punished. Whatever the reason, the monsters all grabbed Andrea's limbs, holding her into the air. Scott backed away in horror, making sure to look over his shoulder frequently to check the front yard.

The monsters ripped Andrea's clothes off as she wailed in horror, begging them for a mercy that she would never receive. "Please, no! God, no, please don't do this! The boy is there! Take him! No!" Her last no was elongated as she was slammed to the ground, brutalized, and then dragged into the backyard. As she disappeared into the darkness, clawing at the ground in a vain attempt to prevent the inevitable, Scott sobbed. He had no time to help, no time to think, and no time to feel. He just had to move.

    Scott ran to the driveway, and unlocked the car. He put Jason into the back, and climbed into the driver's seat. He started the car, floored it into reverse, and set off down Derby Lane towards Market St. He looked out at the stores lining the main strip of his neighborhood, and off in the distance, he saw a faint orange glow coming from his neighborhood. He knew the Hell house was burning down, but he did not care. He just continued driving. Down Market St. to Vista Ridge Ave., and from there to Corral Dr., and from there to Highway 17, and he drove. He drove and he drove until the sun rose up over the horizon. And the entire drive, he did not once take his eyes off his son, who was asleep in the backseat. Not once did he stop thanking God that the nightmare was finally over.

    It was a very long night, after all.

When this portion of the research project began, the list of sources we looked into to piece together this horrific chain of events that haunt the Dunnhill family even to this day began at a truck stop in Vampland, TX. At approximately 8 AM, witnesses say a man stepped out of a car matching the description of that of the Dunnhill's to pump gas and use a telephone. Inside of the car was a severely physically abused little boy passed out in the back seat. People being who they are, the police were called to the scene, and Scott Dunnhill was arrested for child abuse, child endangerment, and driving without a license.

Scott Dunnhill is serving two life sentences at the Sam Kind Correctional Facility in Fort Dalton, TX. Other charges leveled against him include arson and murder. The charred remains of one Christopher Maxwell were found in the rubble of 312 Derby Lane. While initially difficult to have visitation with Scott Dunnhill, the federal research grant caught the attention of Senator Robert Fielding, who took quite an interest in the subject of abnormal psychology and the supernatural. Using his connections, Senator Fielding saw to it that we have extensive time to interview Scott Dunnhill. After an initial period of skepticism, Professor Perry James Alton became convinced that Scott's story was in fact true. That he had done nothing to hurt his son, and that there was some sort of cover up involved.

Jason Dunnhill, meanwhile, was placed in psychiatric care at the Hopewell Wellness Center in Mt. Spruce, Arkansas. Initially afraid to come out of his room, we managed to get him to walk the grounds with Professor Alton and answer yes or no questions. As part of his therapy, Jason Dunnhill was asked to draw anything he desired on a piece of paper. A stack of horrifying drawings, all done with crayon, currently sit in a filing cabinet in the administration office of the Hopewell Wellness Center. Many of the drawings depict things Scott Dunnhill had mentioned in his story: Giant monsters, people in robes, a massive cavern, people being tortured, and a dark altar with a towering monument built of crude, natural elements. It took years for Jason to finally begin speaking in full sentences, and his story was able to corroborate with his father's. Jason's mental and emotional state remain being confined to simple sentences and occasional outbursts of severe panic.

Sadly, Scott Dunnhill is forbidden by law to see or correspond with his son, barring Jason's 18th birthday (provided he is released from psychiatric care at that time).

Naturally, the first course of action we took after speaking with Scott Dunnhill was to investigate the neighborhood. What was once likely a house had been leveled, and the lot had been converted into a garden, complete with benches, flowers, and a fountain featuring the statue of a little boy. It is marked in stone as a memorial to Chris Maxwell, from his loving parents.

According to Scott, the police in Vampland were very interested in what he had to say, however shortly after his arrest, members of a local division of the FBI came in and took control of the investigation. No reason was given, and the Vampland PD's hands were tied. We spoke with the neighbors that Scott had mentioned in his interviews, however many of them, including The Martin's, the Harris's, the Branford's, and the Monroe's, claimed that they did not know the Dunnhill's very well, and that they seemed to be "oddballs."

Our research would not have been able to go anywhere if not for the hard work and dedication of a private investigator named Detective Jeffery Faulkner. Initially hired on by Scott's parents to help prove their son's innocence, Det. Faulkner contacted us shortly after we began speaking to Scott. We shared our interviews with him (he was unable to get in to see him), and he informed us of other such matters that helped flesh out the Dunnhill's story. In particular, the social media accounts of the Dunnhill's neighbors had been scrubbed repeatedly over the years. While they claimed they did not have much interaction, there was much evidence to the contrary, including pictures, video, and metadata linking them to each other at different locations at different times. The records of 312 Derby Lane, while initially sealed by the county, were uncovered by Detective Faulkner (through means which he said were not technically legal). It seemed that a new family would move in roughly every three to six years or so, then would relocate to the same small town in Iowa called Sumner. We searched Iowa maps dating back to the 1950's, however no such town existed.

Detective Faulkner also did amazing work on several child kidnappings ranging back to the 1980's though last year, all within a 150 mile radius of Pemberton. In talking with witnesses who say they'd seen other dark altars, he told us he had found a ring of connected Satanic cults spread out all over the United States. Unfortunately, Detective Faulkner was killed in a plane crash while he was on his way to present his findings at the University of Texas at Pemberton. Professor Alton, who had grown close to Faulkner in the years that the research/investigation was being performed, felt exceptionally guilty, and decided to limit the time he spent on the case.

Before he died, Detective Faulkner spent much time traveling the United States for reasons unknown to me at the time. Prior to Professor Alton officially leaving the project, he informed me that he and Faulkner had a regular correspondence regarding the whereabouts of Andrea Dunnhill. Shortly after the long night at 312 Derby Lane, as the sun rose, police picked up a naked woman, covered in blood, off of F.M. 288, about five miles from the house. Initially refusing to speak, they brought her to the station, where she began rambling incoherently. A deputy who we believe to be unassociated with any Satanic activity recorded her ramblings on a cell phone. When played backwards, the ramblings detail something very sinister:

"It melts away from you. All that is dark is light. You move and then you don't. Time and Space freeze but the new world moves about you. You exist here and there. The realm is the real world, and the old is but an illusion. As you exist, you absorb existence. You crave it. I need more. I need to find the children who will be my gateway into the realm. You call it Hell. We know it to be the birth place of all power."

Shortly after her initial incarceration, there was a power outage recorded at the station at approximately 9:30 PM CST. When the power came back up, the woman we believe to be Andrea Dunnhill (based on description by eye witnesses) was gone. In various counties across the country, a string of child murders occurred under the nose of the general public. Every time, the victims would be drained of their blood and their flesh would be chewed off. And at every crime scene, Detective Faulkner noted the immediate presence of the FBI.

Given his experience of having been a detective himself, Faulkner was good at telling which cops were good, and which were bad. According to Professor Alton, Faulkner would approach the deputies, as he had done in Pemberton, and acquire new bits of evidence that were squirreled away with bureaucratic red tape. Among the most common forms of evidence was a diary seemingly written by Andrea Dunnhill, detailing her life and the traumas she experienced during the long night. Although rough and incoherent at times, there are moments of sharp clarity, painting a picture of a woman filled with deep remorse, fighting off an insatiable hunger.

A woman we believe to be Andrea Dunnhill was found hanging from a tree in the woods near Glen Meadow Park in Riverwood, Mississippi, approximately three miles away from the playground. The words "existence is Happiness" were carved into her chest. All around her, stretching out in a radius of fifty feet, were over a dozen children, originally thought to be missing, hanging from trees. To this date, no known news coverage of this exists.

    As for me, my time being involved in this particular matter must come to an end. I have started a family and relocated to Fort Dalton, and I take much caution from this story. I intend on watching over my son very carefully to ensure his safety. Yet I worry. Like Professor Alton, I take great risk publishing the accounts of the long night at 312 Derby Lane. I have found myself suspicious of any stranger who looks at my son. I am afraid to step out on my back porch at night, fearing I will be greeted by a wall of unspeakable horrors. And yet, I too feel it is the right thing to do. I firmly believe in what I am doing, and can only hope that one day, these matters will be exposed, not as conspiracy theory, but as pure fact. That the public will recoil in horror and question everything they see. And that those responsible for these heinous actions, these elites and locals spread out all over the free world, will be brought to justice in some way. If not for my own family's sake, then for the sake of the Dunnhill's, and everything they had to endure.

Made in the USA
Coppell, TX
30 December 2022

10139172R00067